SAVAGE

SAVAGE DRAGONS BOOK 1

KATHI S. BARTON

This is a work of fiction. Names, characters, places, and incidents are products of the author's imagination or are used fictitiously and are not to be construed as real. Any resemblance to actual events, locations, organizations, or persons, living or dead, is entirely coincidental.

World Castle Publishing, LLC
Pensacola, Florida
Copyright © 2025 Kathi S. Barton
Hardback ISBN: 9798308681090
Paperback ISBN: 9798891263444
eBook ISBN: 9798891263451
First Edition World Castle Publishing, LLC, February 3, 2025
http://www.worldcastlepublishing.com
Licensing Notes
Cover: Cover Designs by Karen
Editor: Karen Fuller

Chapter 1

"Savage!"

"Savage?"

"Savage."

No matter how his name was said to him, it sounded different but never did it sound like anything but a curse word. Sometimes, it felt like that, a curse. Why would anyone name him something akin to a monster? He wished all this time in the new world that he'd been called a different first name than everyone calling him a monster. Not that it would make a difference now. After all these years, he could no more remember his first name, even if he'd had one, than he remembered the faces of his long-lost parents. Not that they had made much of an impression on him as he would have liked.

Savage had been wholly ignored when he'd been born a male. He did wonder, at times, if he'd been hatched as a female, what

Kathi S. Barton

his name would have been. Not that it mattered anymore. The family that he'd had, as well as his first name, was long forgotten.

The poke to his side reminded him that he wasn't alone in letting his mind wander. There were questions that he had to answer and he had a few of his own to ask. Looking at his cousins who had been willing to come with him, he then nodded at them. They were by far the only family that he'd ever had, and even now, he'd lay down his life for them. He did have a sudden thought that if they regretted their last name as much as he did. All of them were hatchlings of one family. The Mercury and Helen Savage grandchildren, who at one time were considered the best family of dragons born to this earth. Standing up, he cleared his throat and asked if it might be heard.

"Mr.....err...Lord Sav..." The man looked at his paperwork. To buy himself time or to look at his notes, he didn't know but he did wait for him to continue. "Mr. Savage, what is your first name for our records?" It was his cousin Kingston, another wonderful name one of them had been given stood up and said that his first name was Tucker. When he looked at him with a questioning brow, he told him that it was as good as any and to claim it. "Thank you, young man. You may proceed, Mr. Savage."

With another quick glare at Kingston, he turned and started speaking to the members of the committee that they'd been called before. They wished to live here, the four of them, but they had to come clean as to what they were. And, in turn, what they could do to benefit the community. Money is what they wanted to hear. They could care less as to what they were, so long as their money was good and they didn't burn down any houses while out and about.

Not that they had a good business plan to help the town help itself. Not with the magic that the four of them had. No. It was just plain, hard earned by their own hands and wit, money. It made him feel dirty when they moved to someplace different. This was through no fault of their own to move halfway across the country was like all the other times they'd had to pack up and leave. Because the land where they'd been could no longer support their lifestyle. Lifestyle? Was it because they were dragons and were a drain on the land surrounding them? It was that they stopped giving out money for every whim that the town had. Supporting causes that only benefited the people in office and their friends. That had been why they'd been asked to leave.

That wasn't right either. It was because they refused to fund the city in what he thought of as robbing them and stopped putting up money for every little project that they wanted. It was draining on them to have to be working hard for money while the cities would continue to grow because of them. No, this time was going to be different. They were just going to be helpful men, and that was all.

"I say there. You seemed to have skipped over my question about funding that you'll put forth for your being here. In order to make sure that our town doesn't end up like others that have dragons in their cities, we're going to have to make sure that there are previsions in place to make sure that we can go on if you decide to leave. Not that we'll not run you out if there is any trouble. No, sir. We want to be assured that there is a town here when things are finished here." He gathered up his things, thinking that there wasn't enough money in the world for him to stay here, when Kingston stood up and pushed him back into his seat.

He was sure that his cousin had just saved the town from being burnt out. He'd had enough of humans in his lifetime. Kingston was much better at calming the beasts that they all had. He didn't understand why he didn't speak in the first place.

"We're just men who happen to turn into dragons. If you're speaking of a monetary donation to the town, we'll be paying our taxes on time. Making improvements on the homes that we planned to purchase. Things that any other law-abiding person would do." He asked him what sort of compensation they'd be paying. "To be honest with you, sir, I don't understand what you're talking about. Do you mean to blackmail us into being able to live here?"

"Yes, you could say that. I want this town to shine, and since I know that you have all kinds of money then I'm going to get as much money as I — where do you think you're going? We're not finished here yet. You people have a seat and listen up to what I'm saying to you. I'm not nearly finished with my demand... my needs. The town needs here." Savage was glad to be out of here. Since they had several places that they'd looked into to live, this was just a mark off the list of places for them to have a nice life. "Perhaps we should start over. I'll listen to your demands, and we'll go from there. Come back here. I want you to stay here, but you must understand that it's not going to be at no cost to the town proper and those who are in charge of such things. Come — "

"Have a nice life." They were all four out the door in record time. He inhaled deeply of the nice air and decided that he was going to find a place that had no pollution in the air so that he could feel like he did right now. Cassian asked if they wanted to get lunch. "Anywhere but here. They'd accuse us of something nefarious, and the only way we'd get out of jail was to agree to their terms. Thanks, but no thanks." The other three agreed that it might be a good idea to leave while they could. There was no point in poking the bear as he'd heard all his life.

They decided on a little diner right outside of town. It was a quint little place and had good portions for the food that they ordered. On the way out, they talked to the owner and decided that if they were in this part of town again, they'd stop by. It was a nice place despite living in the town close to it.

The second place was no better. Once they heard the word dragon, it was all over for them to be living a quiet and peaceful life. This man even told them when he wanted extra money, they'd have to cry for him. He didn't understand where people were getting their information but to cry for gems was only true if they had a reason to create tears. Fresh tears wouldn't produce anything more than tears if there was no emotion behind them.

This man, another mayor looking out for his town, said he had a friend who could exchange gems for ready cash right away. Savage asked if this friend knew about the cost it had on them, and they were waved off in favor of money that all he could get.

It was late when they found them a place to have a meal. Not only that, but there didn't seem to be any place for them to stay other than the bed and breakfast that was in the middle of town. Walking to the only restaurant in town, they noticed that the town was down on its luck. Even the sidewalks needed a good going over or replaced. If the town had charm it was long since gone. The schools looked as if they'd been built sometime in the later century and needed an overhaul more than anything else.

"This place isn't on our list, but it looks like it could use us." Savage agreed with Kingston. "Not to mention the fact that there are signs all over the place that were for a presidential election some years past. Do you suppose they have just given up? Simply don't care if people are here or not?"

"It makes me nervous to think this, but it looks like a ghost town. Did you notice the football fields behind the old high school? It looks like it's not had a game in it for a decade. I don't know if we could help them or simply start over after burning it to the ground. It might be cheaper." He looked at Brenin, who rarely said much, and asked him what he thought.

"I'd be afraid that if they hear the word money or even dragons, they'll suddenly start burning places down to start over. And we'd be taking the blame for it. I'm of the opinion that we let this one slide. It's just too risky for us to step in and help them." He agreed that Brenin might be right. He usually was, anyway. "Do you suppose that they have ever had a single visitor to this place? There wasn't even a single pizza place and we all know that every small town in America has at least two of them. There isn't even one of those ice cream places where kids hang out on Friday night. Nah, I think we should just stick to our schedule. Leave this one to die all on its own."

They ate their dinner and went back to the bed and breakfast. He did wonder why someone would have one in the dead town but didn't ask. The beds were comfortable and clean, and the showers seemed to have the comforts of home. They'd be driving again before the place opened up for breakfast in the morning, so he didn't get a chance to ask the proprietor why things were so down.

It was nearly five when they got up the next morning. They had paid their bill the night before, so they didn't feel bad about leaving before they ate in the kitchen with the owners. He'd bet his last nickel that it was the first time anyone stayed there in a long time. The couple seemed to be unsure as to what to do when they showed up. To help out, instead of sharing a room with each other, they each had their own room which he enjoyed too. It was nice not having to be crowded into a room with someone else for a change.

As the sun was coming up, they were nearly to their next destination. The town was barely bigger than the one they'd only just left but it had nice yards, a couple of churches as well as not just two pizza places but also a place called Dairy Twist. He was going to have a banana split when they were ready to move on, as well as a creamy chicken sandwich. His all-time favorite of sandwiches. Even if they didn't stay here, he'd get his treats and enjoy them very much.

The meeting was set for noon, an odd time to meet with the mayor. When they entered his office, they were all impressed with the setup that greeted them. Not only were there bagels with butter and jams but there was a cooler, an actual cooler of sodas and water there for them as well.

"I'm sorry about the time. But it's my birthday, and the office had me a nice breakfast this morning. I'm so full I'm about to pop." He liked the mayor and thought perhaps they could get a good deal from him. "My wife looked you up, Mr. Savage and was told that you and your brothers—" He corrected him, telling him that they were cousins. "Oh yes. I knew that as well. Yes. But she said that you were wealthy and have been in the market for some time for a place to start your businesses. If you don't mind me asking, why here? We barely have enough teachers to work at the schools. The last time the heat bill came for this building, we had to pay it over time. What I'm saying is, we have very little to offer men like yourself."

"We just want a quiet place to live. And enough land that would be used for a plant like the one that we had where we came from. Businesses that will be able to hire people to work at it and make a good income. There will be perks, too. We'll hire only locals or, if need be, as close to locals as we can get. A staff for our homes. We'll be either building or buying, depending on what is available." Mayor Glenning was nodding as he spoke and seemed to be excited about the prospects of them living there. "We all have different projects that will require a great many employees and land to fill out with factories and manufacturing plants, too. Not just for building a business but for working the lines that will be needed."

"I say, that's a good deal. I have to ask, why did you think it necessary that we know what it is you have planned? Why not just move in and do what you wanted anyway?" He told the man and he seemed confused. "Yes, well, we know what you are, gentlemen. I'm sure that in this day and age, there will be plenty of people coming into towns all over who aren't fully what they seem. Why, I myself am a wolf. I knew that you were different, but not what you are. Being a dragon is something new to me, but not a deal breaker on if you wish to live here. I'm doubting that we'll have any trouble with you and I know, other than a few people that live in town, you won't have any trouble with us either."

Before leaving the office, Mayor David Glenning not only told them of land that was for sale but also hooked them up with his wife, who was the only realtor in town, more like the county as she seemed to be when they looked around.

"We'll have a nice relationship. And so long as you boys don't cause us any trouble, I see no reason whatsoever that there will be any trouble with us either." That was yet to be seen, but so far, he wasn't getting any vibes from the office workers or the Mayor and that was fine by him and the others.

They shook hands on the deal and were invited to his birthday party at the local gym to 'meet and greet' the people that they'd be neighbors with. Sally, the mayor's wife, would have some listings for them to go over as well. The four of them agreed that they'd be better off meeting the towns people as well. It would be very telling, Savage thought, to see what others thought of them being around.

~*~

Two of them found a house that they could live in, which surprised Kingston. One of them, the one that Brenin decided on, was a great antebellum of a place, and he fell in love with it as soon as he saw the wrap-around porch and empty hanging baskets around it. It had a charm to it that his cousin dearly loved, and he could see him there if he got the house. He liked things warm with faded colors in a place.

While it hadn't been lived in for some time, he could see the potential from the car and knew too that it was going to need a great deal of work to bring it up too livable standards. So long as Brenin was happy with it, so was he. The home that he picked out was one that had been considered the mayor's home at one time.

It was large and had lots of room for entertaining. Whether it be indoors or out. There was a nice inground pool that would also need work, but he was fine with it all. It was going to need a staff about as large as his cousins, but they'd get that going when it was time. They were all very good at taking care of themselves as they had been most to all of their lives.

Cassian and Savage were planning to build. The two of them each had thought about buying a condo they could work from until their homes were built and that was fine with them. But in the end, they stayed with their family so that they could be comfortable when they were lonely.

Cassian wanted modern, something that

would be a great deal of glass and chrome. While Savage decided that he just wanted a house he could live in. Unsure as to what he meant, they all seemed to be happy at their choices so long as they had plenty of ground of their own as well as a large enough for family — there was very little of them left nowadays — if they wished to visit. There would be a pool for each of them. A good place to cool down at when they were finished flying around. It took a great deal of water to cool off a dragon and an oversized pool was it. Something else that the others had to learn on their own.

He was the only one with their parents still alive. Savage's parents had died so long ago that the memories of them were colored by his parents, who never cared for Savage or his parents. The two of them were best friends and his mom hated that. But it mattered little to him. They were good for each other and knew enough about the other not to cause any trouble. They all four seemed to just fit.

Cassian and Brenin, brothers had a sister that neither got along with. Kingston didn't care for her either but kept that to himself. Margo wasn't just a bitch, she did that very well, but she was very opinionated as well as thinking very highly of herself. She also thought that since she was decades older than them, they had to listen to her woes. And she had plenty of those as well, thanks to her own stupidity and ways.

Kingston had no one left. Like Savage, the two of them sort of raised themselves. They had hatched at the same time, but there was no one around to show them how to shift, much less get along in the world. Kingston decided that was what made Savage so bitter. He'd had parents, but they wanted nothing to do with him.

Savage's parent hadn't died until much later after the brothers had. He'd been put into a room as an egg and left there until he had hatched alone and ready to be taught the ways of their kind. But since he wasn't the girl that they wanted, he'd been left to his own devises and that of the staff to help him live a life as a dragon.

Savage had never forgiven them for that, and as soon as he could get out of the house to make his own way forward, he did so. They had, as far as any of them knew, never contacted Savage at all in his long life. If not for feeling the moment that they were killed, he might well have gone his entire life without them around.

His sister, Lillith, was named in the will, but the poison that had killed their parents had murdered her as well. After a decade of back and forth, he was able to get their wealth, a great deal of it as it turned out, given to him as well as the other lands, buildings, as well as jewels, and gems to be turned over to him. Of the four of them, he was the richest, but you'd never know it to know him. He was as tight-fisted by half again as the others were.

The party had turned out just as they had hoped. They were able to mingle around with the other residents as well as get to know the feel of the town. For the most part, everyone knew what they were and didn't seem to mind — it was Savage who was forever looking for a harsh word from someone who didn't get too comfy around them, and that was all right as well. Whatever he needed, they'd be there for him. Just as they knew he'd be there for them.

They were all cousins, but for Cassian and Brenin, who were brothers with a single sister. They'd been hatched around the same time, all four of them, and had, for the most part, been best of friends since. Savage was the youngest of them all, at least they thought so—no one was around any longer to tell him when he'd been born. If not for the reading of the will, he might not have ever known he had a sister.

He didn't have anyone, either. Before he'd been hatched so long ago now, he couldn't remember much in the details, but he'd been raised by another elderly couple of dragons that faded away not long after he was at the age of maturity. He knew how lucky he'd been in that but there were times when he realized that he was nothing more than Savage was. A bitter old dragon that disliked humans for all they were worth. Perhaps a little less than his cousin, as he could talk to them without snarling at them. However, neither cared for them and would walk away rather than talk to one for very long.

Savage was going to stay with him while the building was going on for his home. He didn't foresee any issues with them under the same roof as they rarely went out with someone, nor did they socialize all that much. Like him, Savage would prefer reading a good — sometimes a bad book when he wanted things to be quiet. He'd not been lying when he told the Mayor that was all they wanted. Peace and quiet.

Plus, Savage was a good person to have around when he wanted someone to eat with. Being single was the hardest when you had a lonely plate and fork in the sink when you finished eating. Also, Savage for as mean as he could be. He was a killer at puzzles and games of memory and chance. He often thought that he could remember everything that he'd read but never asked him. He wasn't one to brag about himself any more than he was, and that was just fine with him.

There were plenty of things that he had to fix before the house could become a home. Mostly, it was cosmetics that would be needed—a paint brush here. Some new windows in most of the rooms. But Kingston found out that Savage was good at replacing windows as well as caulking and painting a room.

He seemed to enjoy the method behind the job and would do two rooms a week. It was then that Kingston enjoyed his company best when they were working together on the house. He found that he was a good man to have around and thought he'd miss him when he moved out.

Meals were fun, too. They both knew the basis of cooking a good meal but nothing too complicated. Kingston found that he could also bake a nice cake that the two of them would share. There were other things that he discovered about his cousin, and he was glad for the time together.

By the second year of having their homes worked upon, Kingston knew there were going to be issues with the town. He didn't talk about them, but if asked, he would have said that they were a lazy lot and that the only way to get them to work was to stand behind them and make them move.

The high school was nearly finished, and even the middle school was coming along. But they had no teachers lined up to work any more than they did the other batch of people coming around to be a part of the town. And to him, that's what it seemed like, they were batches of people that all did the same work — or, in this case, didn't work the same way. It was frustrating, to say the least. More so since the old buildings were torn down and there were empty buildings around the town that no one could use.

The second most frustrating thing was the mayor. He seemed to have been under the impression that they were going to be the ones who worked the jobs of getting anything done. The painting in the old county office was still waiting for men or women to come in and paint the walls after gutting everything. The paint, in the preferred color, had been sitting for nearly eighteen months when it was discovered, quite by accident, that no one had gotten the cans open, and the painting began. Like everything else, it was all half finished and waiting for someone to get the project going. Stupid, lazy people.

Also, David had not hired anyone to do the sidewalks either. The bids were still in sealed envelopes on his desk without anyone knowing who had won the contract. Christ, the walks were getting worse rather than better, Savage pointed out just before opening the bids, declaring the winner, and getting the job started.

Savage had had to hire the survey for the land that he was planning to purchase. Once it was done, no one could decide on a price for it until he put the mayor's wife in charge of it. She would have made a better mayor than her husband by far. And they each encouraged her to move her husband along so that there would be more money coming in. Without getting things done, no one would move here because it seemed like a half-assed town. Good to a point, then petered out at the end. Christ, it was a nightmare.

When his home was finished and livable, Savage did buy himself a condo. In fact, he purchased the entire development. Once he had them overhauled, he did take two for himself and sold the others for a nice profit. They'd been for sale longer than they'd lived in the town, and it was nice that he got them for the price they'd been appraised at several years ago. They were in good shape just needed some new carpets and lawn work to make them look good. It amazed him with a good coat of paint, and a freshly mowed yard could do for a place. However, he loved his home and did miss his cousin living there with him.

Things were moving along nicely once the mayor was voted out and his wife took over. It was good for the town to have someone who was social, too. She would find things in the town that no one would have thought of, and it was good for them as well.

The grocery store was too small for how big the area was becoming. But instead of building onto the one that was there, it was left and a new larger one was put in the other end of town. The older people in the town didn't care all that much for the new place and were loyal to the smaller one. It worked out well for everyone.

Once things started rolling along in a nice way, the library asked for computers from the county. While they could very well afford to put computers in every house in the city, they said that they'd go half on them with the city. For every dollar they earned, they'd match it. Brenin was good at giving suggestions on how to raise money, so he would be found at all the meetings about the program, and in the end, they were able to purchase eight new computers as well as printers to go with them. Everyone was happy, and so were they. It was a good way to start things off, he thought, since they'd been so behind before.

Things were moving along nicely, and

they couldn't be happier. None of them dated
all that much but would, outside the limits of
the town, go and find someone to have a nice
dinner with. Savage, for all his good looks and
lack of charm, stayed home most nights, and
that seemed to be fine with him. He only hoped
that someday someone would come along and
show him what it was like to be loved. If any of
them deserved it, it would be his young cousin.

Chapter 2

Twenty-eight years later.

Kaida watched as the product went down the line. It would mean that until the next set of stores were added into the night, she'd be finished to clean up her mod. It wasn't really a mess, she usually cleaned as she made her way down the product line, but there were still bits and pieces that needed to be picked up that she'd dropped.

They'd send her the labels about an hour after she was finished putting the first set — one on each of the products that she had in her mod. The last batch had her putting a single label on over seventy-three ramen noodle boxes as well as a lot of other things that she had. Mostly, the noodles, but there were things like cases of green beans, peas, and corn. Once, she had a mod full of Christmas paper and that had been several hundred of the labels with a single one to be put on each box.

"Hey, K." She hated the shortened version of her name and ignored the man calling her that. "K? Are you finished with your stores? I need some help."

She turned and looked at him with the powdered donut left overs on his shirt. Mac, his name illuded her for now because she didn't particularly care for the man. His smiled creeped her out a bit, too. Like he was leering at her or something.

"Kaida. My name is Kaida." He told her that was his pet name for her. "It's still Kaida. Not K. or whatever other shortened form of it you come up with. Also, I'm not a pet for you but a woman who has a first name that you can't seem to remember."

"Whatever. I'm behind. Can you come up and —" She was shaking her head before he was able to finish. "I know, I know, you're not supposed to help me out, but I'm going to lose my job if you —"

"The last time I helped you, you'd not

even started on your labels. How many are you behind now that you need help." He told her that he was counting on her to help him, so he'd waited on her. "I'm not going to help you, Mac. Your job is to get your labels out, and if you don't do it, they're going to fire you. I'm finished because I don't screw around waiting for someone to come along and do it for me. Unlike you, I don't take a break from working until it's time to go."

"Come on. We're friends, and friends do things for one another." She began cleaning up her mod and ignored him. He was a lazy fucker and thought he should have been fired a year ago. "Just this one time. I'll be better at getting some out next time you help me."

"No." Grabbing her broom, she was startled when it was jerked from her hands and hit with it. "What do you think you're doing? Get away from me. Stop before you hurt me."

The next thing she knew, she was waking up in the back of an ambulance. Even then, she didn't know what had happened. She sat up and looked at all the blood that seemed to be all over her. Looking at the woman who was sitting talking to someone beyond them, she asked what had happened.

"What can *you* tell me about what had happened?" Kaida replied what had happened right up until waking up a few minutes ago. Just then, realizing that the woman was a cop not a medic. "I have a different version of that from the man who accused you of hitting him."

"Did you look at the security tapes?" She told her the company was getting them for her now. "Mac has been told before that he can't beat people into submission to helping him. They put him on my mod because the cameras were set up there after the last time he hit someone. He nearly killed the last person."

"Like I'm supposed to rely on your word that you were the victim. So get this, on your word alone, I'm going to allow them to take you to the—"

"Margaret? What the hell are you doing interviewing my victim?" She told the man, whom she couldn't see, that she wasn't a victim but a perpetrator. "That's not for you to say.

This is mine and — why hasn't she been sent to the hospital yet? She needs stitches, for Christ sake. Get your ass out of there and let them get her some medical attention."

In a lot less time than she could count, not only was she being taken away, but there was an IV in her arm and a blood pressure cuff on her other arm. Also, before she could ask for something for pain, her body began to need something more than the aspirin she'd taken an hour before work this morning, she was given enough to take the edge off, they told her.

When she was being unloaded from the ambulance, one of the medics was telling her where she was hurt. Every time he listed a place, it began to hurt badly. Especially the ones on her face. Even her eyes felt like Mac had tired to remove them with her broom.

She didn't know what was going on for the first hour or so she was there. Her body hurt, and it felt to her like every question started with her doing something wrong. The little shit had better lose his job after this, or she was going to quit. Kaida had been at the warehouse since before it had opened, helping get the shelves hung correctly and the computer system set up in a way that when it did open, every person working would have not just a badge that would clock them in and out but one that would help them with the flow of their jobs too. Just as it had been told to her, it would.

In the last ten years, she'd seen a lot of people come and go. Especially the management. They thought that with a place as large as it was, fifty-six thousand square foot, they could hide out and do things that were better left at home. Or their car.

She especially loved the rule that there was no smoking on the job. No vaping, either. The place didn't have the terrible smell of cigarettes to the things. It did, however, sometimes in the summer have a very strong smell of body odor when the breeze from the large fans were working. Sometimes, that alone would make her wish she could hand out the little containers of deodorant to the employees rather than not being able to tell them that they stank.

"Ms. Loren?" She'd only just gotten back from an x-ray when there was another person in her room. She told him that it was her, but she wasn't feeling up to answering any more questions right now. "I understand. I do. But I need this one question answered. It's for insurance. Did the management know that Donald MacKenize was a problem before transferring him to your mod?"

"Yes. That's why they put him on my mod. So that when he got behind, I could catch him up. After that, he started waiting for me to put his labels on the product to be sent out. I told them several times that he's been in trouble three other times that I know of for beating up a worker and that I wanted double pay if I had to do his work in addition to mine. They thought I was funning them. Do I look like a person with much of a sense of humor? I'm not." She closed her eyes and laid back on her bed. "I'm really beaten up here, buddy. I'm off tomorrow, but I have to work the day after, so if you'd not mind, I'd like some rest time before my next shift comes up."

"How long have you worked there?" There was something about his voice that had her resting better than with the sound of hospital workings. After telling him how long, he laughed. "What is your employee number, if you don't mind me asking."

"Two. It should have been one, but that number was taken when the equipment I was testing failed to print my picture. I'm the only one, other than the big boss, that is still left." She yawned and heard him chuckle again. "Go away, will you? I have to get stitches soon, and I want this to last. I've never felt this relaxed since I was born, I don't think?"

Another chuckle and she didn't have the energy to look up to see what he was laughing at. She couldn't even see him all that well because of the bandages on her eyes and face. He must have been a loon. No one ever thought that she was funny even when she had the jokes explained to her. After another laugh, she was out.

Kaida was being shaken awake sometime

later. The room was semi dark and the sounds were different. Asking whomever was in her room what they were doing, she was told that they were getting her blood pressure. She wanted to tell them to be more quiet but she was awake now so it mattered little. She asked the woman the time.

"Just a little after five." That was usually when she got up so didn't bitch about being awake. "You'll get to go home today if you have someone that can stay with you. Is there anyone you want me to call for you?"

"Not unless you can raise the dead, then no." The girl asked her what she said and she told her that she had no family to speak of. "They've all disowned me or written me off long ago. It's doubtful that I could pick them out of a lineup either."

"All right then. I'll let the doctor know." She started to leave but turned back. "You should call your breakfast in now if you're ready to eat. They'll start getting busy when the rest of the patients get up in about an hour."

Kaida wasn't all that hungry yet but

she knew that skipping meals was as bad as over eating. You were fucked either way. As soon as she hung up the phone, a man came into her room and started barking questions at her. Some point in his lecturing her about how things were going to go, her breakfast arrived and she tossed half of her bagel at him. That got him to shut up.

"What the hell was—" She told him her name and put out her hand to get his name. There was rudeness, she was good at that, then there was just plain being an asshole, which it seemed to her he could have cornered the market on. "Savage. I think one of my cousins said my first name was Tucker."

"You don't know your name?" He said it had been a while since anyone called him that. "I see. So you go by Savage. Is that your trademark, Mr. Savage or have you, like Tucker acquired that name from one of your cousins. I do hope that you don't leave the office too much or you'd be shit out of luck with your mannerisms coming out so pleasantly."

"You're not so nice yourself." She told

him that she never said she was. "All right. I'm guessing that now that we have the pleasantries out in the open and you dislike me as much as I do you, but I own the business that you were hurt at and I want to get to the bottom of how it happened."

"I'm fine by the way. Since you didn't care if I was or not, maybe you should get your information from Mac. His name, in the event that you'd care is Donald MacKenize. His employee number is eight thousand and twenty-three. That's how many people have been hired and gotten rid of since I've been working there. Mostly it's management. You might want to put that on your to-do list as to why you have such a high turnover. I know but it's best if you find it. I get into trouble by 'nosing' into places that I shouldn't. Which makes no sense either as I'm the only one that knows how to operate the machine that prints badges." He asked her why. "Why you ask? That's another thing you might want to put on that list. Why am I training all your management on how to operate the machinery — including and not limited to the fork lifts and stoles that are used here daily. When they're out the door a few months later. I don't teach them to work here. I train them on the operations part but not the management part. That's where they're failing. Or someone is."

"You seem to know a great deal about my business." She didn't even blink at the man but let him figure that out for himself. If he could. "All right. How long has Mac worked there before yesterday, and who is his direct report to."

She gave Savage the answers and more information than he might need or not about both men. Kaida thought that she might know more about the employees there than any one person in Human Resources did. She was good at remembering details and information like that. Anything that she'd read or seen as a matter of fact. Kaida could just remember it.

After three hours she was ready for her lunch and a nap. Her temper wasn't any less volatile than his was but she was enjoying putting him in his place when he got nasty with her. He was there because he needed her, not the other way around.

"You said that your first name is Kaida. Do you know what it means?" She told him. "Little dragon suits you more than I think the person who named you is aware of."

"Same as you, Savage." When he stood up and stretched, she looked away. There was more to him than the owner of the company that she just happened to work for and it had her body tingling in places she'd not thought of in months. "Are you about finished? I need my lunch and to find someone that I can stay with tonight. With the concussion, they don't want me passing out when I get home alone."

"You'll stay with me."

~*~

Savage was still trying to figure out what made him offer up his home and quiet to the girl. She was ruder than he'd ever come across in a human. It also startled him when the more she bulked at the idea, the more he fought in telling her that she was going to do what he said. Like he actually wanted her to stay in his only breathing space and quiet on this earth.

It wasn't until he had Kingston talk to her that she finally agreed. Telling her some bullshit about her being under their care because they owned the company and didn't want her to sue them. Sounded plausible to him, but she was still bitching as they were getting ready to transfer her over to his home.

"You could have just left me at home, you know. I can no more afford to sue you than I can put a downpayment on a house. That's all I'm working for. A home with a little picket fence around it for me to let Geoffrey out." It was Kingston that got out of her that it was her only friend and a cat that cared for her. "He seems to think that the apartment that I live in is his, and I'm the persona non grata that he graciously allows to live with him."

"Cats don't care for us." She glanced at him when Kingston laughed. "You'd be wrong about them not liking Savage. All animals love him. I think he has a couple of dogs and three or four outdoor cats hanging around his barn now, too. I think there might have been a squirrel and a couple of snakes that have taken to hanging out at his home."

"Figures about the snakes." No more was said as they got her in the car. Since he was the only one who drove, they all had licenses, but he was the one who had the most experience with it. He drove her to his home. It gave him time to think about the twit in the back seat of his car.

She wasn't just a smart ass but a clever one as well. He thought she could stand toe to toe to any of them and come out the winner. None of them were barred from her sharp tongue or wit either. For whatever reason, he found himself thinking up things to say to her that would get her going. Or to touch the temper that he knew she had.

His cousins decided to stay for dinner. Not that he minded all that much. The house could certainly hold them all for dinner. But like he'd been doing, they seemed to tweak at her to see what she'd say next. Like it was a challenge to see who could get blasted by her first. None of them had, so far, gotten her as angry as he did, and was glad for that.

She begged for a nap, and they all left her to it. As she stepped into the room, he could see her concern or whatever one might encounter upon seeing a room decorated just so. Savage would admit this to no one but he hated the room and most of the house too.

He'd had a decorator come and finish up his home after it was built, and he hated every part of it. The room that she was in, the blue room the woman had called it, didn't have a spot of blue in it anywhere. And she had thought that it was funny. Not to him. If it was the blue room, then it should be called that because it had too much blue in it. Not devoid of the color on purpose.

When his cousins all left an hour later, with the promise of coming back for dinner, he wandered around the house looking into the places that she had commented on. Like the blue room, she had questioned his use of no color in the opening entrance hall. It was all white. Even the vase and flowers that were all plastic or some other shit that she told him that he should be ashamed to call it an entrance. An entrance into what? Hell, she'd asked him.

"The stairs to the second and third floor were, in her words, 'hooker red' like the place you'd find in a 'brothel that handled prostitutes and madams.' He didn't know why, but that was all he could see now that it had been pointed out to him. Savage decided that she'd be as good as him when it came to crossword puzzles. There were other references as well.

The front doors were off-center. He'd known that when the place was built and thought that he could live with it. As soon as he could get to a phone, he was going to have that fixed. He didn't know how much that bothered him until then.

In addition to the front hallway and stairs, there were the rooms that were just off from the room. The library with all the books turned the wrong way as well as no pictures were annoying. He had plenty of them, so why didn't they get to be hung in his own house. He was going to get onto that as well. Also how the hell did he ever find a book the way that they were. Savage simply ended up buying another copy if he needed a book he knew he had because of that.

The office doors were closed, and he was sure that she'd have something to say about it. He did. Plenty. All the equipment, the printer, the safe, and the terminal were all hidden behind walls. To make it appear as if he didn't do much work in the room. That was the only thing that the woman had gotten right. He couldn't work in the room at all. It took him a month in the room to know that he did indeed have a computer. He just had to dig it out of the desk that he hated as much as he was beginning to hate the house.

Savage hadn't been happy with the house when he'd had it built. There wasn't anything wrong with it other than it was way too feminine for his tastes, as well as too many things that were not up to his standards. It didn't help either that he'd fired the decorator before she was finished with it. She had told him that the house needed a woman's touch, and she was going to be the woman that touched all the shit in the place for him. That, more than anything, had soured him to the place. That and the fact that it was at the wrong angle to the street — his mind seemed to close down when he heard his name being called.

Taking the stairs two at a time, he was standing in the blue room in seconds. Just in time to catch the little dragon before she fell. Shaking his head at her foolishness in trying to get up, she smacked him across the face before he could make her understand that she needed to be more thoughtful in getting around. He asked her what she'd hit him for.

"Because every time I talk to you, you're yelling at me. Couldn't you just not this one time? It's the reason that I didn't call for you before getting up. I fucking hurt, and I have to pee. Go away if you're going to yell all the time." Savage heard the words out of his mouth before he could realize that he'd never once said them to another human being in his life. "I'm sure you're not sorry, but worried I might be suing you or something. Christ, I have a headache to end all headaches, and I still have to — put me down, you moron. You'll hurt your back carrying me around like that."

"Hush. You don't weigh much more than a dragon's egg." He didn't even know why he'd said that to her, but telling her that he was sorry set him on edge. "If you can manage not falling on your ass long enough to go to the privy, then I'll take you back to bed when you're finished."

"Go away." He left her to her business and stood in the room waiting. He looked around and thought that this room had all the character of a puppet with no hand. Like the front hall was devoid of color, this one had it all — except blue. He wanted to find a can of paint and fix that before he did anything else. The clearing of her throat had him turning and scooping her up into his arms.

"What were you mumbling about? And if it's about me, then shut up. I don't want to feel any more depressed than I am right now." He asked her if it was the room. "As a matter of fact it does have a bit to do with this room. It's the ugliest room I've ever been in. Who the hell thought that bright green paisley could go well with black and white Poka dots. And who puts vertical blinds on short windows? Someone blind did this room, or you did. You didn't, did you?"

"No. I actually paid a heartless woman to do this room up and call it blue. There is none. Trust me, I looked hard for it." She agreed with him as he was putting her on the bed. "I'm sorry that I was barking at you. It's what you might call my calling card. I don't like humans."

"I'm assuming that you are something that isn't." He told her that he was a dragon. "Good to know. Do you, by any chance, eat humans for your meals?"

"Not for a long time." She seemed to act like he was serious, so he let it go. "I'm not a large dragon. I could easily fill out this house with my other self but that would be a waste of time to have to—but to think on that, this house might well be better off being torn down and starting over."

"You paid someone to build this for you too? Are you a sadist?" She laughed when he did. However, his sounded rusty and out of place to even himself. When he leaned back in the chair again, she really took the time to get a good look at him. He didn't mind. It gave him the time to look at her, too. "You're not as young as you appear either, are you?"

"No. Several thousand years older, to be honest. My cousins are all older than I am, but once we reach a certain time in our lives, we no long age. Up until recently, like in the last couple of decades, I didn't know my first name. I don't know where they came up with Tucker, but I needed one, and they told me to use it. I only use it when necessary." She said that she thought Tucker suited him better than Savage. "You don't know me all that well, though."

"True." She looked at him again. "To me, you look like a man that has spent his life being bitter about humans and really could give two shits if one of them killed you or not." He said that he couldn't be killed as his dragon at all and that, as his other self, there was only the one way. "Pierced through the heart or losing your head?" He told her. "Yes, well, that would kill me as I'm only a human. Where are your lovely parents in your life? I'm betting that they're lurking someplace to take advantage of you before they try to kill you off."

"They're dead." She was embarrassed and told him how sorry she was. "They never cared for me and once they realized that I wasn't the girl they had wanted, then they faded from my life. Or abruptly left my life. I'm not sure which is true. I think they're the ones that called me Savage in the first place. We were all descendants of the Savage line, and we, back in the beginning, were considered the most savage of all dragons. I guess I still am. All of us are. You've met Kingston and Brenin, I think. There is also Cassian. He and Brenin are brothers. They have a sister that they don't have a lot to do with. Her name is Margo."

He told her about his family and how they'd been killed along with his sister Lillith. He told her how he'd heard they had died since he'd never known much about them. He wasn't too sure.

"I could feel their deaths. I guess other

shifters can do the same. But I didn't bond at all with my sister. She's much older than I am. I didn't know about her until they were told to me from their attorney. He knew I was out there, and it was several decades before he could find me to give me their wealth."

"Do you have a lot of that? Wealth, I mean?" He nodded, which seemed fine with her. "I have about twenty grand in the bank. I'm waiting for a house, any house that doesn't mean fixer-upper to purchase. I've been close once or twice but never been able to sign on the dotted line." She looked around again and asked him if he'd really had this place done the way that it was.

"I did. It's ugly, I know. Every time I pass one of the rooms that have been left open, I don't go in but close the door to it. If you think this is all wrong, you should see the master suite. It's hideous." Again, the laughter but it seemed less harsh this time. "I was going to go by and feed your cat for you, but all we have on file for you is a post office box number with no forwarding address."

"That's all I gave them when I started. I did live with my parents when they were killed, but once I turned eighteen, my uncle had me move out. I was in the middle of my senior year when he did that to me. Anyway, it's all water under the bridge now, and I have myself a nice cozy one bedroom flat that Geoff shares with me." She laughed. "If he could hear me talking about him, he'd be pissed off. What am I saying? Everything pisses him off. I think he only tolerates me because I buy him food. Otherwise, I don't think he'd care a fig if I were murdered someday on the way home from work. I guess like it nearly happened."

"You'll be happy to know that the place is under new management. Mac has been arrested, and his court date is in a couple of weeks. You were correct in telling us that he's been up to this for a while. Why they kept letting him work it beyond me." She told him what she'd heard. "That makes sense, I suppose. His aunty being the wife of the plant manager. They're all gone as well. Most of the management staff is by the way. None of the employees as yet but that'll be up to them if they stay or not. Now that I have an idea what was going on, I've dug deeper into the paperwork to find out all kinds of things."

"I only know a few of the employees. There are a few that I don't understand how got into the door, but perhaps the plant manager's family is running the show instead of him." They spoke a bit more until he could see that she needed rest. He was fine with her taking a nap. He felt like he needed one as well.

Chapter 3

Savage was still sitting at his desk, a horrific thought of sitting here all day, when his computer signaled that he had a message. Pulling it up, he nearly snarled at the computer when it told him the message was from the new mayor. He wanted to get with him and talk about the new projects that he had in mind for the town.

Brenin joined him just as he was ready to tell the other man that he had plans too then wanted to ask him if he wanted to come to those meetings about his house or not. Lucky or not, Brenin asked him to delete the message and wait for him to take the email.

"I have a question for you." Before his cousin could ask, Savage told him his plans for getting rid of his home and starting anew. "Good. That was my question. If you were ready to start looking for a new place. Not a new town. I don't want to move from here but just start fresh in our own lives, like a new home or something like that. Something that takes us out of — hanging around Kaida has given me a fresh outlook on things. Her no-nonsense attacks on things make me think outside the box, so to speak. When she speaks her mind, it makes me feel like she's rattling my own mind in opening my eyes to things I've never seen before."

He looked at Brenin and thought of his own arguments or talks with Kaida. Leaning back in the chair at his large desk, all he could think about was how much he enjoyed just hanging out with her. Sitting up abruptly, he narrowed his eyes at Brenin.

"Little dragon." Brenin told him that he knew what that meant. "No, I mean...she's my little dragon. My mate. At least, I think so. I didn't get what the big deal was when, just yesterday, she told me that she was healed from all the wounds that Mac gave her. She seemed to think that it was a big deal that she was nearly healed with very little scarring. I just wrote it off because that's what happens to me. But...Christ, Brenin, she's my mate, and I didn't even realize it."

"How do you think she's going to take that? Last I heard, the two of you were fighting over something about her going back to work." He said that he wanted her to get her home before it was too late. "Oh, so you told her to spend her hard-earned money on a home so that she can enjoy it before she dies. Good one, that. Did you part with any more information about her impending death that you shared with her?" He snorted. "Gee, little cousin, you have a knack with women, don't you?"

"She didn't take it that way." He thought about her anger with him and thought perhaps Brenin was correct. She had been out of sorts with him. "I'll let her pick out the house that we'll live in, and that will make it up to her. Don't you think?"

"I think if you continue on in the way that you are, you're going to be a lonely dragon longer than we will be." Brenin snapped his fingers. "I'm going to take notes about you.

How not to treat my new mate so that she doesn't remove my head before I get it out of my ass and make her happy."

"You're insufferable. Did you know that?" He just laughed and let him sit in his office. Savage was fine with that. If he didn't have anything better to do than to make fun of him, he could go home. Savage decided to go and find his little dragon. Let her know what a fine life she was to have now that he was a part of it.

It took him most of the afternoon to look into places he thought that she might be. Then, another hour to find her in the backyard of Kingston's home digging up herbs. Apparently, she found some she didn't have in her extensive window garden at home.

"I've been looking for you all day. You seemed to be avoiding me." She said that she'd been doing things that she normally didn't when she didn't have any time off from work. "Well, you should have told me."

"Why?" He didn't have an answer to that and told her she should have known that he'd be looking for her. "Why would you be looking for me? I have shit that I have to do now that I'm going to be dying soon. Isn't that what you told me. That I should get on the stick about living my short life?"

"I did not say that. I only pointed out that if you didn't buy your home soon, you'd not be able to enjoy it all that long. But that's not right now. You'll live a long life now, thanks to me." He wanted her to be excited to ask him what he meant, but she only turned from him and began putting her little plants in the containers that she had with her. "Perhaps you didn't hear me. I said that you'd be living a longer life because of me. Aren't you interested?"

"If I pretend to be interested, will you go away? I have things that I'm doing." He told her this was important. "So is what I'm doing. Tell me or not. I'm busy right now."

"You get to be my mate." She turned then and looked at him. When she stood up, he thought that she was finally getting on board with what news he had to impart with her. The punch to his face knocked him back some, and he was pissed about it. But one look at her face and he thought perhaps that he'd been right about her last week. She didn't understand the workings of a dragon. "Let me explain this better to—"

"Oh, you've explained this well enough. I get to learn a whole new life in living with you as your mate and I should be thrilled beyond words that you figured it out for me. Did you think that I was too dumb not to have figured it out before you did? I did. I've known for at least since the day after we met. I tried several times over the last few weeks to give you hints, but you just didn't get it. I guess it only means that I get to be your mate. Isn't that what you said because you finally got your thick head out of your ass and figured it out on your own? Christ, you're stupid. Not only that, but you don't seem to have one lick of manners in your whole body that would make a woman want to be with you."

When she started to storm off, he backed away from her when she came back toward him. But all she did was pick up her little plants and carry them to the little basket she had by her water. The growl, low and full of anger, had him taking a few more steps back until he was flush with the barn in Kingston's backyard.

It was the first time in his life that he'd ever been afraid of something smaller than him. Even when things were larger than he was, he knew as a dragon that he was much meaner and stronger. But this little slip of a female human had his dragon backing up and his entire body feeling like he might well live longer, at least not hurt as much if he were to leave her to her business of picking herbs out of the yard. He was certain, too, that if he brought up the fact that she was his mate again, she'd remove his head with a swipe of her hand, magic or not. She seemed ready to do him bodily harm for some reason.

When she left him standing there, Savage fell to his knees. His heart was pounding, and his body felt like he'd run a great long run in just the few minutes that he'd been standing beside her. He had a little thought, one that he was determined to keep to himself. He was not going to cross words with her again. She was much too dangerous.

The rest of his day he tried not to think about Kaida. But he would find himself at odd moments not only thinking about her but holding the phone in his hand to call her. Each time, he put it down quickly in fear of him somehow connecting with her. He could not believe — yet he did too — that she had brought such thoughts of him being powerless and her being the one that held all the magic. Magic or not, he knew that she was going to catch him unawares, and he'd be toast.

After contacting another realtor, he had him looking for him several places where he could live. He would have asked Kaida for her input, but frankly, he was giving her as much time as she needed to get in a better mood. Not that he'd say that to her, no way, but he would tread quietly around her until then.

Women were just odd, he told himself. Why was she taking things out on him, for Christ sake? So what if she'd figured out before he had that she belonged to him. Why didn't she thank him for it instead of making him go all over the place looking for him? Women? Why did a dragon need a mate in the first place? Of course, to have more dragons, but he didn't think that was a forever thing. His parent certainly never were around for him.

But then he was bitter about that, too. He couldn't really make up his mind in what he wanted anymore. Did he want a mate? Not particularly. But he didn't want to be alone either. It was scary at times when he was alone. Thoughts of finding someone to remove his head or to kill him as a human were forever invading his thoughts. He was lonely, even with his cousins around at times.

There were other times when he wished he could find himself a cave and live out the rest of his life there. He wondered what Kaida would think about that and decided that she would probably be just fine with him living out his life in a cave. It would be without her, for sure. She would be just like that.

Savage was of the opinion that he didn't

know what he wanted. He liked hanging out with his little dragon a great deal. She was funny and witty. Mean, sure, but he liked that too. Perhaps there was something wrong with him? Maybe he was off his own rocker and needed his head removed because of that. Savage had no idea. Whatever it was, he knew that she was the one that was causing all the trouble he was having.

He realized that she was standing in front of him in that very moment and asked her what she wanted. It took him several seconds to realize that she was crying, and he hurt him on a level that he didn't understand.

"What's the matter with you?" He didn't like the sound of her crying. It did all kinds of things to his chest and heart. "You're crying. Stop that right now."

"Do you have one pit of compassion in your chest at all? I mean, is it your norm to go around snapping at people when they come to ask you a question?" He asked her what she wanted. "I wanted to know if you're right and that I'm going to die soon? How much time do

I have left?"

"I told you that you don't have to worry about that anymore. Because you belong to me, then you'll live as long as I do. When I die, it's said that your heart will be so broken that you can't stand to live without me and die too." She told him that she might well hurry him along to death to test that theory. "Why are you forever testing me? Sometimes it's all right, but there are times when I just don't care to have you around."

"Well, that feeling is mutual. Do you suppose you could cut out being so fucking honest all the time and just answer the questions nicely? Doubtful, but let's see. I was wondering why you hate me so much? Try not to say the first thing that pops into your head." He said that he didn't hate her, just didn't like that she was human. "All right. Since I can't change the fact that I'm human, what else do you dislike about me?"

"Actually, you're not human anymore." They both turned to Kingston. "I would have called out when I found your door open, but

I heard the two of you arguing again. As for you being human, the moment that you met Savage you were no longer human. You have magic that he might well have shared with you that neither of you realized. Also, you might well have things that we've shared with you because we're related and older than him. Not much, mind you. A couple of hundred years, but it might be something that you got from us."

"I don't know if you realize this or not but a couple of hundred years to me is a long time. What kind of magic?" He pointed out things that she'd already figured out on her own, like healing quicker. "So if I were to fall and break my leg, it might well have healed better than it would have a couple of weeks ago?"

"Did you fall and break your leg?" She said that she thought that she might well have when she was at her apartment this morning. "Climbing around might not be such a good idea until we get things figured out. None of us have a good handle on things about mates and how they are taken care of by us. So hold off on doing things that might get you otherwise killed, please?"

Kingston had Kaida try a couple of simple magic things that they could all do. She could heal herself easily. Also, if she wanted something like a glass of water — the simplest thing that they could think about, she could make it appear as well. Other things too, the simple magic of making sure that she could be found and will herself to someplace else. He'd only had her go to the next house he'd been thinking of buying, but she wouldn't give him any kind of opinion about it until he did her. Women. They were all just too complicated.

~*~

She agreed to go on the house-hunting trip with both men. Kingston was calmer than Savage was. He was also easier to talk to. Sometimes, he'd get into it with his cousin, but since it didn't involve her, she just let them go at it. To her, their arguments were sort of stupid. Who cared who had the most scales or had done something several hundred years ago that the other didn't. She was just glad to be not at work.

Which she was going to go to tomorrow morning. They'd called her back this afternoon, and she was actually looking forward to having something normal again. Not that she'd seen their dragons, but hanging out with them wasn't all that fun. They argued too much.

Then, there were the feelings that she was beginning to have for the stupid dragon. Well, all of them were nice, but Savage was something more. He'd sent her to her room in tears on more than one occasion. At least once a day, she thought. Then there were the times that she wanted to simply bash his head in and be done with him. Knowing that wouldn't kill him, she wondered if he slept with one eye open and watched for her to come and remove his head. For all she knew, he slept in the yard as his dragon just to keep her from doing him bodily harm.

Wandering off from the two of them, she entered the kitchen to find that it wasn't even up to the last couple of centuries. Someone had tried to salvage the room, but it was too far gone to do much more than to tear it out to the studs and start over. She thought that the entire house needed to be done that way. Kingston asked her about the house.

"One of you should shift to your dragons and burn it to the ground. It's not worth the money that one might pay for it, even if it was only a couple of dollars. It doesn't even have enough room for the refrigerator but for the small one in the corner. I don't need to see the rest of the house to know that no one has done a thing to it since you guys were born." She turned to look at him. "What does Savage say?"

"Nearly word for word what you said." She shrugged and turned to leave the room. "You're in love with him, aren't you?" She didn't have it in her to lie to the other man.

"I don't know what I feel for him. Other than I want to break his neck most of the time and others…well, there isn't much difference in how I feel about him in any way. He's not nice to me, and yet I find that I want to be around him for the once in a great while nice things that he can say." Kingston nodded. "What does that mean?"

"It means that he feels something for you, I think that he's in love with you but terrified that you'll leave him when he least expects it. Or perhaps he'll expect it daily. I don't know if it matters or not but he has never loved anyone but us. And at times, I'm sure that he thinks that he's incapable of love." Kaida said that was sad. "It is. And while I've never met his parents I'm sure that they were just as incapable of love as well. Did you know that he had a sister?"

"I heard him talking to you guys about her. She must have been a real diva." Kingston laughed and said that was her in a nutshell from what he'd heard. "They all died from a poison, I heard. I didn't think that was possible."

"Only as a human was it. I think that it was someone from the pageantry that she was in. They were forever winning something for her beauty. I never met her either but I've heard that she mostly used magic to make herself beautiful. Sad really. Savage is a great man and could be a better mate to you if you were to give him a chance." She asked him if he was blaming her for him being an asshole. "No. Gosh no. I only meant that you could change his mind on being a good-minded person if you were to… well, bash it into his head what an ass he is. I'm sure you'd have no trouble with that."

"Are you saying that I'm mean?" When his cheeks pinked up, she laughed. "I was only kidding. But I will admit that he hurts me in ways that I've never hurt before. It's like he's out to destroy me."

"Perhaps in his own way, that's what he's doing. To destroy any kind of love you might have for him because he's never felt anyone love him before. And if he keeps you at arm's length, just to keep himself from feeling anything for you—at least acknowledging it, he'll not have to hurt again like he did with his parents." She didn't know his parents but could easily hate them for the damage that they did to him. Kaida said as much to Kingston. "No truer words could be spoken. As I said, I've never met them but from what I've heard, they were never kind to anyone. Not even each other. My parents didn't like them, nor do they care for—they actually hate Savage. I don't have any idea why. I don't know that they've ever met him, but they didn't care for his parents, and I guess they figured that he was just like them when it couldn't be further from the truth." Savage joined them in the kitchen and said that he'd lost track of time.

"I was wandering through the house and decided, if that's all right with you, that there is nothing redeeming about this house. Not only is there no charm, but it would be better off left to rot or to be torn down and rebuilt." She told him that she agreed with him. "Good. Now, we have three more houses to look at but I'm starved. Let's go get something to eat and then move on from there. The realtor has given me the codes for the next houses so that we can take our time. Philly isn't at all like her mother, Sally Glenning, is she?"

"I don't know her. I'm sure it was before I was born." They both laughed then Savage asked her how old she was. After telling him that she was twenty-seven, he agreed with her in saying that she hadn't been born. "Gee, thanks."

The three of them decided that they'd eat a light lunch and then go from there. She didn't know what they would think of a heavy lunch for what they ordered but they ate a great deal if you were to ask her. She had a taco salad, and they ate two large subs apiece. Plus fries which was something that she had never cared for. Having her fill, it was Kingston who finished her salad and they were off again. This was trying looking at places, but she was having fun as well.

They didn't even go into the second house on the list. From where they were sitting in the car, they could tell that it was no better than the first house. Savage hung up the phone and said that he bought the first house in order to tear it down.

"While I don't know what I'll do with the property, I know that the land will be worth more without that eyesore sitting on it." Kingston agreed and told her that land wasn't plentiful, but houses were. She supposed that made sense. It wasn't like there would be any more land made around the world.

The final house was the kind of house that she'd dreamed of owning her entire life. It was a little larger than she would have hoped for with having six bedrooms, but the yard was large, and there was even a fenced in back yard for the dogs that she wanted. The wrap-around porch was wide and well-maintained. There were even hooks to hang baskets of flowers if she wanted.

She was nearly giddy with the prospect of touring the house. Even if Savage didn't purchase the home, she was going to. It even had a place for flowers to plant in the front of the house that she wanted. No fence, but she could easily do that on her own.

There were minor things wrong with the house once she got close enough to look at it. There were places on the porch that needed to be repaired before someone went through the flooring. There were also a couple of windows that were broken out and she could see that someone at some time had boarded them up.

Inside the house was wonderfully exactly

what she wanted. A large kitchen with an eat-in area. And herb window over the sink that looked out over the expansive backyard. There was a pool to which she liked, but the hot tub was a nice addition as well.

"You like this one?" She nodded to Savage and told him that if he didn't buy it, she was going to. "Will you allow me to live here with you? I can easily pay cash for it, but I have a feeling that you'd hit me if I were to suggest such a thing."

"You're right. I don't know that I have enough for a down payment, so if you'd like to live here with me then I'll have to ask you for help in the mortgage as well. And don't pay cash for it. That hurts the economy if you were to do that." He told her that he would do whatever she wanted. It took her several seconds of staring at him before he asked what he'd done now. "You're being odd again. Have you had a change of heart or something? Or did you grow one?"

"That was just mean." She told him she was sorry and that she'd been used to him being mean to her. "I guess that's right. You might well see me be mean again, but I'm working on it. You make me want to be a better person."

"I don't know that I've done anything of the kind, but I appreciate you being nicer." They toured the rest of the house, and she loved that it wasn't perfect. It would be something that they could — or she could work on between her shifts at work. She'd have to keep her job now, as she had a house payment to take into account even if he were going to pay half of it.

As she had no idea how to make an offer, Savage did it for her. When the realtor called them back within minutes, she was worried that they were going to turn them down. Instead, they had a counteroffer of less than they offered just to get it off the books. She'd not realized that it was part of a bank repossession and was thrilled when it came back at about half of what they'd offered.

As the house had been empty for some time, Savage hired a crew to go in and clean the place from top to bottom. There were five bedrooms, including the master and she was thrilled that he wanted to keep things just the way that they were. That way, they could move right in and be enjoying the house sooner. She'd never once in her life lived in a house without wheels, and she was thrilled beyond reason that she was getting her dream house in this one.

"We'll need to get something to fill it out with." She asked him if he had anything from the other house that he wanted. "No. Christ no. I hate everything about the place. We can either donate what is there if we can't sell it of burn it all for all I care. It's the most hideous house I've ever lived in. And I lived in caves that had more charm than that one does."

She laughed. It wasn't long before she felt herself relaxing around him, and that made her nervous. As soon as she let her guard down, she knew that he was going to attack her again. Keeping her emotions to herself, she asked him if he had some kind of storage which he kept his old stuff in.

"No. I think that Brenin and Cassian do. Did I tell you that they're brothers? Hatched on the same day from what they've said. I don't know if that makes them twins or not, but that's what I've heard from them. They also have a sister too, Margo but they have very little to no contact with her." She asked him about Kingston. "He might have everything he owned in the house that he has now. I don't know. But he's looking for something new as well. I think that we all are. Not a new town but new homes."

The rest of the afternoon into the evening they measured and took notes on the house. Kingston left them so that he could work on looking for houses, too. Savage told her that he thought that they all needed a good change for now. They'd been living in their homes for the past thirty years and had had enough.

He'd been right. They had been around here longer than she'd been living. It saddened her to know that she wasn't going to have anything to compare her life with his. He'd seen so much that he more than likely could tell her stories of his life that would make the hair on her arms raise up and tingle. Shaking her head, she continued on with the house to make sure that whatever happened in the future, she was about as prepared as she could be about it.

However, she wondered if her heart could be prepared at all for their departure. She was nearly about as in love with the man as she was with anything she'd ever felt before. Kaida wondered if being in love with the big dork was going to be anything that she could recover from once he decided that he'd had enough of her like he did his home. Him moving on scared her to no end.

Chapter 4

Kingston answered his phone without looking at it. It had to be important enough to call him, he thought, but regretted it the moment he heard his mother's voice.

"Are you still hanging around with that savage?" He simply closed his phone without speaking to her. When she called back again, she also reached out to him. He decided that he had better things to do other than speak to his mom about his best friend and how he was such a pimple on the Savage name. *"Answer the fucking phone before I have to come there. And you know what will happen if I do. I want you to hear my voice and hear how disappointed I am in you."*

"I don't care, and if you want to come here, go for it. I'm having dinner with Savage tonight. He has a new home, and the rest of us are going to help him celebrate." For some reason he thought it best that he didn't mention that he'd also

found his mate. She'd start in on—something occurred to him, and he smiled as he spoke to his mother. *"He has a mate now. Not one that you'd want to mess with however. She's called little dragon and sometimes scares mine and the others dragons even though she's human."*

"Human? Christ, I knew that he was going to sully the name of Savage more someday. I've said this before, but I think that instead of putting him in a dark place to be hatched, his parents should have destroyed him before that time. I didn't like them, but there was no reason for them to have left the rest of us with him." He told her that she was going too far. *"What are you going to do about it, Kingston? Come after me? I doubt you have the balls for that. And so you're aware if you so much as think about having a human as a mate, I'll...I'll disown you."*

"Then I'm hoping now that she is human. Just so I don't have to put up with these monthly calls. Mother, you couldn't do anything about him before he became my friend, and there is very little you can do now that he is." He took in a deep breath before continuing. *"Is there anything*

else? I have a great deal going on here, and you're keeping me from it."

"I'm your mother, and you'll give me the respect that I deserve." He told her that she was lucky that he was giving her any respect at all for as much as he disliked her. *"You're a terrible son. Nothing like the others."*

"Good. Sucking up to you isn't anything that I enjoy, but that's fine too." He wondered what others she could have been talking about since he knew he'd been an only child. *"You have a good life, and know that if any harm comes to Savage or his mate, I'll kill you. Laws or not, you will perish by my hand even if I must go to prison for it."*

He closed the connection tightly and didn't allow her into his head again. She was a horror, his mother and his father wasn't too much better. He also knew that in a couple of days, more than likely less, he'd be hearing from his father on his treatment of his mother. Fuck them both. If they came here, which he was thinking that they would, he'd have to deal with them face to face. Fine with him. Kingston wanted to see their faces when he told them he was out of their lives. He only hoped that before they arrived that he'd have a human mate. Just to —

Kingston didn't care for the way his thoughts were going. It hurt him a little to think that he'd been wishing for a mate simply to piss off his parents. As far as he was concerned, especially after meeting Kaida, he couldn't wait to meet his own mate. And hoped that she'd put him to the tests the way that Kaida did Savage. Him, too, if he was honest with himself.

Brenin was about half in love with her himself. She'd scolded him once the other day about going out in public the way that he looked. Sweat pants and a tee shirt that he was sure that was older than she was. She told him that if he didn't have respect for himself, how would he get respect from others. Brenin went out that very day and bought him some new clothes, something that he didn't think any of them had done since moving here. Not when they could make their own clothing appear and disappear with a thought. When his phone rang, he didn't answer it.

Whomever it was, they'd left a message, and he listened to it. It was his attorney telling him that his parents had been inquiring about his worth. That he should call him back if he wanted more details. He did in that moment.

"I've spoken to your mother once and your father twice. They seem to think that you're broke." Kingston asked if they still thought that or did he tell them. "I told them that I couldn't discuss it with them unless you allowed it. That was your mother. Then your father called me to tell me I was to do what she wanted or he'd have me fired. I'm not worried about them."

"I'm thinking that they're on their way here soon." He said that he'd keep an eye on things here and would let him know if he saw anything. "Thank you. She is going on about Savage again. And now that he has found his mate, he's even worse than he was before."

"If you don't mind me saying so, Lord Savage, your mother isn't sane." He couldn't help it, he laughed. "Anything else I should know?"

"Yes, I nearly forgot about what I called you about. There are four homes that are surrounding your parents' home that have come up for sale. If you want them, say the word, and I'll get them for you. You know as well as I do as to what sort of neighborhood they're in. But to be honest with you, I think that the entire place is going downhill. There aren't a great many improvements going on there, and I hate to say it, but your parents haven't done anything to their house in over a couple of centuries. And their yards are so overgrown it's almost jungle like. There is a company that does their lawns, but I don't think even that is being done properly."

"Get me the houses and make it so that the lawns are done up, and the houses are in good shape. I'm not opposed to making them rentals just to piss them off." He laughed when he thought of his mother's thoughts on renters. "Let me know what you find out, and I'll go from there."

It wasn't twenty minutes later when he heard from Scott again. His parents had contacted a private plane service. Scott was laughing so hard that he could barely understand him.

"They wanted them to do it for free." He told him how his friend owned a couple of private jets that he flew others around in. "Just because they are the great and — they actually said this to him, the great and powerful Savages, and he could advertise that he flew them to their son's home for advertising. I nearly wet myself when he told me that."

He enjoyed his laughter. "I'm assuming that they might be flying commercial then?" Scott told him that he would let him know. He had friends there as well. All right, but I should be preparing myself for them as well as the others."

"Something that I've been meaning to ask you. You said that Savage has a mate. Do you know if he's going to put her name on his homes? As I told your parents, I don't discuss other clients with anyone, but he has a substantial amount of money he needs to talk to her about." He said that he'd ask him. "I will tell you this. He has a great deal more than you or your cousins put together. He hasn't done anything with it since he's gotten it."

"I'll talk to him. He might not understand that he needs to keep investing." Which he didn't believe was true. Savage might be as mean as he was, but he wasn't stupid either. "Are you handling his money?"

"My brother is. He asked me to say something to you so that he can work with his funds. It's not like it's sitting idle at all, but he could be doing so much more with it." He thought about Kaida and her starting back at work tomorrow. "You'll not get into hot water with him, will you? Don't do it if you think you might."

"I'll think about it. Maybe with him having a mate, he'll be a little more free with it. I know for a fact that he's forever worrying about money. I think that's why he works so hard, afraid of him running out of cash or something. He's been like that all his life." Scott said that he could well understand that, too. "I bet you can. All right. Keep me informed about my parents. I'll let everyone on this end know that they're coming. I don't know how they feel about Cassian or Brenin, but they'll need to be warned as well."

The first person that he thought of was Savage and Kaida too. Mom would be gunning for him and it wouldn't do well to have her causing trouble with Kaida either. He thought that she could hold her own, but she was only partially human and she would hurt her given the chance.

After contacting Savage and letting him know, he could almost feel his mind working and his temper getting the better of him. Then, almost as if someone had touched him, he calmed down. It had to be his little dragon, as he'd been calling Kaida all along. He was invited to their house for dinner along with Cassian and Brenin. That way, he could warn them all at one time and that would be just what was needed. The sooner, the better.

"Also, I talked to my investment attorney.

Do you have one?" He told him that he worked with David Jameison, brother to Scott. *"Good. Have you thought about what you need to have Kaida put on your deeds? I don't know how much you need to do with that or even if you wish to do that. But she's going to need to know what sort of money you have so that she's not as stressed about it as you are."*

"I think that she'd kill me if I suggested that. I have been thinking that I need to do more with my inheritance, but I've been hard-pressed to find the time. You know, Kingston? It's really strange having a woman around all the time. And what's even odder is that I find that I want to be with her even if I've pissed her off about something." He told him he thought he was odd, too. *"True, but she's calming to me as well. I don't know if that's normal or not, but just her touching my shoulder a little bit ago, it took all my anger away just like a snap to your fingers. It scared me a little too."*

Kingston and the others were going to pick up food to bring to Savage and Kaida's home. They had ordered a table and chairs for the dining room and it had already been delivered. He wondered what he'd do about the rest of the house and decided that he'd have a good time picking things out with Kaida. She'd put her style on the rooms that he knew would please them both. He also knew that the colors would be earth tones, like most of the clothing that she wore, as well as serviceable furniture that would last a long time.

By the time he was ready to pick up the food he'd been assigned to pick up, he'd heard from Scott two more times. His parents were coming tomorrow on a private jet as well as that Savage had contacted David about several things and was putting Kaida's name on everything. That sounded like a large undertaking, but said nothing to Savage about it.

By the time the others had shown up, he had talked to the two of them like he'd never done before. Seriously, and without joking around. Telling Savage that his parents were going to harm Kaida got him upset. Savage said that he'd protect her with all that he was from them. Kingston had no doubt that he would, too. And that Kaida would do the same for him. They were, it suddenly occurred to him, a perfectly matched couple. Both of them were no-nonsense when it came to saying just what they needed to at the perfect time. And doing what needed to be done for the family. And she was as much family as Savage was.

Dinner was wonderful. They'd not gotten together like this in a very long time. It was good for all of them, too, to know what Savage had to say about his parents and what sort of steps he was taking to guard himself and Kaida. It was no longer hurtful when Savage told him how mean his parents were. Nor saying what he was going to be doing to them when he saw them.

"But I promise you this, Kingston, I will not make a move toward them unless they do to me and mine first, and that would include you and the others." He nodded, knowing that even before he said it. Savage was true to his word, too. More so than most men that he knew. "We'll know how to act when they get here. Hopefully, they'll come, say what they want, and leave."

"Do you believe that? That they'll just come here and tell us what they think of things and leave?" Savage asked what he thought. "I don't know. I wouldn't put anything past them at this point."

"Then we're going to be ready for them when they arrive. Whatever happens, when they do get here, will be all on them." He agreed and decided that his parents were going to be on their own from now on. They'll either leave on their own or not, but it was going to be entirely up to them.

~*~

Kaida watched the couple coming up the runway. For some reason Kingston's family had asked for them all to be there at the airport. It was funny to her that they had demanded that they all be dressed in finery, whatever that meant to an older couple of dragons. And they were to be respectful. Only if they were would she be respectful.

Savage had told her enough about them that she wanted to hate them on sight. But there were Kingston's feelings in this and she didn't want him to be hurt if she were to be nasty to them. She didn't want them around, not at all, but it wasn't her call.

Yesterday all their furniture had arrived. It was just as wonderful as she'd thought it would be. Even today, while they were here, a white picket fence was being put in and she was so excited that she wanted to stay home to be the first to see it. Silly, she knew but that had been something that she'd been dreaming about for years. It was going to be epic living there with Savage. So long as he kept his temper under control.

Last night, after everyone had left, he sat her down and went over his finances. With the help of his attorney, David, she now had a good grasp on how much he was worth and how many homes he owned as well as businesses. She knew how much he was worth and, in turn, she was worth, but it was still circling around in her mind about how many zeros were in the amount. It was something that she didn't believe there were numbers for. But she had smiled and nodded like she was some sort of simpleton. This morning, she was given a handful of credit cards, keys to a nice new car, as well as dressmakers coming tomorrow after Kingston's parents arrived to fit her for some nicer dresses so that they could go out when they wanted.

It was nearly too much for her.

She watched as Kingston's mother was barking orders at the people around her. They were busy carrying bags, and such with them, and to her, it looked like they were planning to stay for a long time, if not forever. As soon as she was within touching Kingston, she drew back her hand to slap him, she thought. Instead of allowing that, Kaida grabbed her hand and held it.

"We'll be civil around here. Isn't that what you said? And if you draw back to slap him or anyone here again, I'll rip your arm off and beat you to death with it." She smiled at the woman but she was far from humored. "My name is Kaida Loren Savage, mate to Tucker. I'm thinking that I'm going to be calling him by his first name from now on. He's not a monster, no matter how many times you say that to him. And I'd keep a civil tongue in my mouth about that as well."

"You dare touch me? You're nothing to me. Do you hear me? Nothing." Turning on her heel, she started to leave the airport. The men would follow her or not but she wasn't going to be embarrassed in the local airport because some broad was having a hissy fit. "Where do you think you're going? Kingston, get back here right now. I demand that you treat me the way that I deserve."

"Oh, trust me on that, Mother, I'm treating you better than you deserve. Right now, you could say that I'm giving you a few feet until you calm the fuck down. And yes, I said that. Now, either you keep your trap shut, or I'm going to close it for you. I'm finished with you treating those that I love like they're nothing beneath your feet."

Someone touched Kaida on her shoulder, and she turned to look at Tucker.

"I have fallen in love with you. I think

I might have been all along, but when you grabbed her hand and told her off, I nearly fell over. My love for you hit me so hard." She stood there and opened her mouth, unsure as to what to say when Kingston caught up with her. He too told her that he loved her but she wasn't sure it was the same. Catching up with Cassian and Brenin on either side of her, she was in the limo, and on her way to the home she shared with Tucker before the older couple got out of the airport proper. "Are you all right?"

"I don't know." Tucker nodded. "Do you care if I call you by the name that Kingston gave you? I could go back to Savage, I suppose, but I'd rather not."

"I'd be honored if you'd call me anything other than Savage. Thank you for your help in dealing with the Savages. I don't think that it's finished yet, but you sure showed them what you're going to be tolerating or not." She said that she didn't want her to hit her friend. "Nor did I, but you handled it a good deal better than I would have. The airport is still standing, thanks to your way."

Just this morning, Tucker had shown her his dragon. He said that he was smaller than the others because he was a fire dragon and they were not. She'd not known there were different kinds of dragons, but the others were white dragons. They could breathe fire a little bit, but they mostly used their huge bodies to destroy rather than burn. Brenin told her that was because Tucker was more powerful than they were. Not only could he burn through almost anything, but he was bigger than other fire dragons as well.

"What are you thinking about, love?" She told him about his dragon and his fire. "I would never harm you. Not intentionally. You must be, as I said to you before we left be careful around me. My tail sometimes had a mind of his own and will whip out when it thinks to."

"I remember it's size." She also remembered the spikes along it. The dark, blood-red scales that covered it to the end. She, at the time, had been intrigued; now she knew that, above anything else, he'd protect her with his dragon. No one in her life had protected her from anything or anyone as far as she knew. "He's beautiful. I wish now that I'd taken his picture. No one would believe that you're real, but I would know."

"Perhaps next time." She nodded and laughed when he pulled her closer to him. "They will fight dirty when it comes to getting what they want. I don't know what that is other than they want Kingston to come back to their home with them but they will stop at nothing to get that. Did you notice the other woman with them?"

She looked up at him, concerned they were already causing trouble. When he told her the woman was Cassian and Brenin's sister, Margo, she felt her hair dance on her arms and her body chill. She'd heard what sort of person she was, too, and she was by far worse than the other two.

Cassian told her that when he'd been born, she tried to pull his wings off. Kaida hadn't known that when a dragon was born, it was a dragon no larger than a human infant. Then, when his brother had been born, she tried her best to chase him around the house with an axe, wanting him to die as well. Their parents had done nothing about it, saying that she was simply teaching them how to be better dragons when they grew up. Cassian told her that all it had done was make him more leery of his sister than most were of their worst enemy.

As she got older, her methods of trying to kill them off got more dangerous. It was why, as soon as they could, they left the nest in favor of raising themselves. It was that, or Margo was going to kill them in some way, and that would have been a great loss to her. Even in the last few years, she'd tried to kill them. Or to maim them in a way that she could take care of them. Kaida didn't have any family, but she thought that they'd have been better than Margo was to her younger brothers.

They found out that the Savages and Margo with them were going to be staying in town at the local hotel. It wasn't a grand one, barely called a hotel but it was quaint and close to downtown. They were perhaps only about four blocks from Cassian's home and even closer to their own. It was yet a few more blocks to Kingston's house and he wasn't sure if they thought that he was closer to them. Perhaps even living in the house that Tucker and her were living in.

"What about sex?" She nearly fell over she had turned so quickly to make sure what Tucker said. After asking him, he laughed and told her what he'd said. It wasn't that funny of a subject if he asked her. "I'd never rush you, but I was wondering if you would allow me to sleep with you from now on. I won't harm you in any way nor take advantage of you. But I'd love to feel your warmth close to us, my dragon and myself, with the others around."

"Is that really why you want to sleep with me?" He said that he wanted to make love with her as well, but he'd be happy with just holding her. It would make both him and his other half happy to know that she was close when something went wrong. "I suppose that's as good a reason as any other. However, I will tell you if you get it into your head again that I belong to you, I'm going to hurt you in ways that you've never dreamed of."

"Trust me when I tell you that I'm well aware of that. And that you could hurt me. But I also want you to know that you hold my heart in your hands for as much as I love you." He got down on his knee and looked up at her. "I've been a fool. A cruel man who only looked at you as something and someone that I would have to care for. Never taking into consideration how much you would give me in return. With only a look or a thought, you could render me useless. Have me rethink my life choices and what I've been up until now."

"Get up." He put something in her hand and kissed it after closing it. "You don't have to do all this Tucker. I said that you could sleep with me."

"I didn't do this before I asked you because I didn't want you to think that I was blackmailing you into something. I love you, Kaida Loren Savage — I fell a bit more in love with you when you called yourself that earlier. But I have this for you that I made so long ago that I nearly forgot it." He opened her palm and she got a look at the ring—such a mundane word for the piece of jewelry that lay there. "The base is made of my scale and will magically size to your finger when you wear it. You don't have to worry about it breaking, either. It's made of my other half and will not only not shatter when hit, but it will protect you from harm as well."

He slipped it over the first knuckle, and she smiled at him. It vibrated around her, and as she watched him push it more onto her finger, she could feel the magic of it running up and over her arm to her own body. And it did fit like it had been made for her. It was the most beautiful thing she'd ever seen.

The band of it was wide and so brilliantly shiny that she wanted to hold it up to the sun to see it sparkle around her. It was the blood-red color of his dragon and it too seemed to catch all the sunlight that was shining down on them and sparkle in the eyes of both her and Tucker.

The diamonds were set in a Tiffany setting that showed off the gems like it was an offering to her. Even the blue sapphires were bright. She did lift it up to the sun and laughed when it rained beautiful stars around her to the point that she was dizzy with them. It was like she was being rained upon by the most wonderful colors in the world, and she couldn't have been happier.

"I'm glad that you like it." She asked him if anyone else had worn it, hoping not, but didn't know. Her trust level in the man was still new to her about him. "No one but you would wear something so beautiful as you are. It dulls in beauty when you wear it upon your finger." He pulled out the second, much larger band. "This is for myself, as I want everyone to know that you have chosen me over all men in the world. I will forever be your one and only from this day forward."

His words were like a branding to her heart. They were there for her to pull out and think on for all her days. This day to her would be like none other. The day that Tucker Savage had chosen to take her as his mate forever more.

"I love it, and I love you." He kissed her hand again and stood up. "Will you kiss me and sort of seal the deal between us? I don't care for a fancy wedding or even a small one. Just knowing that we're together will make me the happiest woman forever. I love you so much, Tucker. But if you get all macho on me again, I will not hesitate in taking you out. I won't be hurt by your words or actions again. Do you understand me? I won't give you a second chance with this. You either keep your mouth shut when you want to be mean, or I'll remind you what it's like to have words hurt you."

"I understand." He pulled her into his arms and lifted her chin up. "Kaida. My little dragon, I love you so much." Then he kissed her, making her body feel heat from the bottom of her feet to the top of her head.

Chapter 5

Margo hung up the phone and let a little of her dragon go to let off steam. She'd been warned no less than a dozen times that if she messed up the room, she was going to have to pay for it. The Savages were making her life hard at the moment, but they had allowed her — well, she had bullied them into bringing her along. Christ, even her brothers were turning against her. Smiling, she thought that was funny. They'd never liked her any more than she liked them. Being their older sister had made her angry at the time, and it hadn't gotten any better when they were older, either. She had loved being an only child, and her parents paid for them having the two boys with their lives.

Plus, her needing to make sure that they knew who was the stronger of the three of them had paid off over the years. She had always bullied them into her way of thinking, even going so far as to make sure that they were the ones who had been caught when things went sour. Sometimes, she would just walk away and leave them to face whatever consequences there were when she wanted them to suffer. Yes, she thought to herself, they were going to give her what she wanted and then beg her to allow them to live.

Never one to save money, she was in deep trouble now. If not for Sofia and William, her aunt and uncle, she would have been jailed a long time ago. She might well have known that there were fees and dues to the leader of their kind owed, but she'd never paid any attention to it or the summons that she'd gotten either. She'd never been responsible for anything. And even if she had been, it didn't take long for her to shove it all the way to the back of her mind and right out. Being responsible for things would mess up her life.

Now she had less than thirty days to make it right, or she was going to be stripped of her magic and her dragon, pretty much killing her where she stood. It wasn't fair that they could kill off dragons and when it came to her, it was suddenly frowned upon. Stupid rules. She hated to have to be ruled by people. They should just let her have her fun, damn it.

With pentiles and back payment she owed her kind nearly fifty million dollars. Then there were the other things that they were attaching to her bill. Attorney fees for them having to find her and calculate how much it came to. There were also the damages that she caused when they brought her in. Shifting to her dragon at that moment had gotten her nearly killed as well.

"They're going to pay it all for me and keep their mouths shut too." She thought about seeing Savage there. "Christ, what a delicious hunk of waste of a man. She might not have alienated him so much if she'd known that he'd be that good-looking later in life. Her brothers were so-so looking, but Savage looked like the name that he went by, a savage and a good-looking one, too.

Now, all she had to do was get ahold of her brothers and shake them empty of cash.

Maybe getting an eye full of hoping for more than she needed, she was going to take that as well. No longer was she going to be without just because she didn't have cash or gems on her all the time.

Her usage of tears had been taken from her when they thought that she'd killed her parents. She had, but without proof, all they'd been able to do was take a bit of her magic away. She had disliked her parents as much as she had her brothers. Well, anyone if she was honest with herself. Sometimes, Margo didn't even care for herself, much less a bunch of humans gathered together in one place. Christ.

The older her parents had gotten, the more set in their ways they became, like humans, only worse. They'd even gotten into the habit of hanging out with humans. Having vacations with them and the like. Killing them had been her greatest triumph. Nothing could have pleased her more than being able to tell the world how easy it had been to murder them in their beds one night. The worst part was, of course, that since they had thought that she'd killed them, she couldn't inherit their fortune. She wondered if her stupid brothers had ever realized or been told that they had a great deal of money left to them by their parents. The fools would give it to her if she was able to tell them. God, how she hated them both so much.

Her phone ringing startled her out of her thinking, and she snapped when she said her name. Whoever the person was on the other end was laughing, and that pissed her off even more. Hanging up seemed the right thing to do, and she'd be willing to bet that they'd call her back within minutes of realizing who they had angered. Putting her phone on the little table she had, Margo waited for whomever it was to call her back.

Three hours later, they still hadn't called her again. Thinking that it had been the perfect way to show someone how not to be on her bad side, she still wished, just a little, that she knew who had called. It couldn't have been one of her brothers. They would know better than to not call her back not to mention just talking to her in the first place. They had to know that it would piss her off.

Nor the Savages, Aunt Sofia, and Uncle William. Even though they'd not wanted her on this trip with them, they had gotten her a hotel room without room service. She'd tried to order something, just to test the waters, so to speak, but they told her that unless she had cash, they weren't bringing her anything to eat.

"Mother fuckers." She didn't know what to think about her aunt and uncle when it came to Kingston. He didn't bother them. Never once did she ever remember him being disrespectful to them, with the exception of the airport shit. But the way that they were speaking on the way to the little hotel, it had been planned that the other woman would show herself by being mean to Kaida. "Sofia seemed to think that the little twit was going to own them something, too. For some reason, I'd not mess with the stranger. She seems to be slightly deranged."

William brought up how she was human. Only human is what he called her. Maybe they were hoping for her to be only a human, but she was far from that. You could almost smell the magic surrounding her. And it was powerful, too. While she didn't think that she could shift, it would only be because she didn't want to. The woman was scary like that. And she did wonder, off and on today, what she was doing with Savage. He had said, mate, but that could have been a lie. Neither of them had rings on, so that was just bullshit, she told herself.

Time would tell when she met up with her brothers. They'd tell her all she needed to know before she beat them senseless. She couldn't kill them, mores the pity, but she could hurt them in ways that she'd never used on someone before. Having them dead would mean that everything they had, and she was sure there was plenty to be had, she'd get it all and be worry-free for the next few centuries or so. Poisoning her parents is what got the law put into effect that you couldn't kill those related to you by blood. She'd been skirting around that law her entire life and had gotten away with it time and time again. Just look at Savage's parents.

Kelly and Ben had been all right as an

uncle and aunt. Savage had never been in the picture when they came to family outings, and he'd been less in the picture when she killed them. Had she known about the money that they had, she might well have killed them sooner rather than later. Before Savage and Lillian were born.

They deserved to die after using their magic to make sure that Lillian won all the awards for her beauty and poise. She'd asked to be able to be competitive with her cousin, but she was told—even today, it still hurt her that she'd been told that she wasn't nearly as beautiful as Lillian was and that they didn't have time for her. That got them all three dead. Treating her like she was an ugly duckling had pissed her off enough that when she'd killed her aunt, who had said that to her, she killed off Lillian as well as her mother. Kelly wasn't beautiful at all when she got done with her nor was Lillian. It made her smile when she thought of how much pleasure she got out of the way that she'd murdered the three of them and got her to laughing when she thought of her uncle Ben telling her that she had broken the law by killing her relatives and that he was going to turn her in. Like that ever happened.

She was startled when a woman answered the phone when she tried to contact Cassian. She said hello twice before she asked if this was Margo Savage. She told her that it was before she could remember that she was all badass, and the woman on the other end of the line was —

"This is Kaida Savage. What do you want calling your brothers twenty times in the last half hour?" Again, startled out of making a good comeback, she really felt her dragon react to the woman's laughter.

"I want to talk to them, obviously. They are my next of kin." The laughter again. "What makes you think that you can do anything with me. I'm nearly ten times your age not to mention, I'm a dragon that eats your kind for breakfast."

"Yes, I've heard about how you treat your next of kin. Did you really try and kill the two of them when they were only days old?" She said that she had and then told her they were going to die soon enough by her hands. "We'll see about that. I know you think you're all that and a bag of chips, but I'm in charge now, and you're going to have to come through me to get to them."

"Gladly." She felt a moment of fear when she remembered who she was talking to. But once more when she thought of the magic around her, she remembered that not only were her brothers there but her aunt and uncle, Savage and Kingston. They were the reason for all the magic that she had felt. "Why don't we get together and hash out how I'm going to murder you as well."

"Sure. And good luck with that, killing me I mean. I have something that is going to protect me, as well as the love of four of the greatest men I've ever met. They can kill you if you harm or speak of harming anyone that has yet to do anything to you." She asked her where she'd gotten that drivel. "Oh, from the laws governing your kind. Mostly its you that I'm looking things up on. And something else you didn't understand, if I draw first blood, you and your dragon belong to me. Did you read that little tidbit?"

"You lie." Kaida asked her why she'd lie to her, as she had nothing to gain. "You'll need to come here now and meet me. If you do, then I might even allow you to watch Savage die before I kill you. That'll be fun, don't you think?"

"You'll be happy to know, too, that I have a few things up my sleeve. I've been playing around with the magic that I got from the men and realizing that I have a lot of it. It's funny, really. You'll never be able to get away from me once I see you." Margo laughed, but she was nervous. If she was reading up on— "Yes, in reading your mind, I have contacted the committee and told them where you are. For now, they're letting me tangle with you, and when I'm finished with you, they'll get what's left of you."

"Brave words for a human." At least, she hoped she was human. But again, the more she thought about it she knew that it had been the others around her. "You come on here and allow me to tear you up."

While on her phone, her door was knocked on. Since she'd been able to trick the staff into bringing food for her aunt and uncle, she was going to be in the hall when it arrived to take it into her room. She just then realized that they had been knocking on her door when she opened it. The slice to her cheek had her falling to the floor. She was owned by someone else. And it was Kaida Savage if she didn't miss her bet.

"Sit in the chair over there, and don't make a sound." She did so, crawling on her hands and knees until she was all the way across the room. Getting up to sit, she put her hand on her cheek and remembered something else about the law. She would not heal until she was allowed. Even then, she'd still only answer to Kaida and never have a thought of her own until the day she died. Or was killed by her. "Just so you know, you really fucked up with me."

"Yes, your ladyship." She hadn't known

that the other woman was a lady until the words flowed from her mouth. Even then she hated to know too that once she said that status, she would now have to call her that forever. Again, until she died. And since there was no blood between the two of them to make them related, she would be able to kill her as well. Margo was well and truly fucked. Her brothers walked in just as she was thinking of plans to get out of this. "What are they doing here? Will you allow me no dignity?"

"You mean like you did for them? No. And because I've read the entire book of laws that you should have been well versed on, I'm going to turn you over to them so that they can do with you what they wish, including but not limited to killing you. They can do what they want with your body and that of the dragon, too. You should have been more up on your laws, Margo. You might well have saved you from being treated the way you treated them." Laughing, the woman left the three of them there. Picking up the phone, she heard Brenin order several large pizzas and something to drink. She knew too that they'd not share with her and she wished now she'd been able to get the food that was coming to her aunt.

After they ate all eight pizzas and drank nearly a twelve-pack of beer, the two of them sat and watched television without allowing her to turn to see what they were looking at. After the silence of the TV being turned off, they came to stand in front of her.

"You'll forever follow us ten steps behind us with your head lowered and your hands behind your back. You'll wear what we tell you, eat what we allow you, as well as going to bed, on the floor when we allow that as well." Cassian grinned. "You fucked with the wrong woman, Margo, and I couldn't be happier."

So, her life began as a slave to her brothers. She knew the humiliation of what she was going to endure for the rest of her days, and there was nothing that she could do about it. Margo was royally fucked over.

~*~

After telling Tucker what she'd done, she was happy that he laughed. Every time he asked her a question about how her brothers were taking it and Margo's look on her face, he'd laughed all the harder. She thought that he was getting good at laughter. She especially loved it when he laughed with her. His sense of humor was much like her own, salty and harsh.

When they went up to bed later that night, she got into bed first. For the past three nights, they'd been sleeping in the same bed, and Tucker had been true to his word. Only sleeping with her throughout the night. He even made the bed when she got up before him, and she thought that was the sweetest thing in the world. The man was a charmer. Who knew?

Kaida had never slept with anyone before Tucker. But she had seen naked men, mostly in art class when she'd taken a few college classes, using the male form as a model. But Tucker was different. He was muscled and hard, his skin was silky and tight. And hot. Everywhere she touched him, she felt his heat.

"It's my dragon. I've had the occasion to touch the others with their dragons and they're not nearly as warm as I am. In fact, they have to stay warm in the winter months as their bodies can't take the cold like I do. That's why I was so happy that we have a pool. It's the only way that I can completely cool off in the summer months by taking a long soak in it." She asked him if it would be too hot for her to swim in after he had cooled off. "I never thought of that before. We'll have to test it when I use the pool again. I know that I create a steam bath in the bathroom when I take a cold shower." Kaida didn't even ask him why he was taking cold showers. She thought that she might well know.

Deciding that she had enough of just sleeping with him, she was going to mark him as hers. Or the other way around. She really didn't care right now. As soon as he was in the bed, his boxer briefs were the only thing that was keeping them both completely naked. She started touching him as much as she wanted to.

Moving her hands down his hard abs, she ran her fingers through the coarser hair just below his belly button. His hiss of pain or pleasure, she didn't know which had her looking up at him. His eyes, usually a lovely shade of blue were darkened to a nearly black color. His nostrils were flared like he was trying to get in whatever scent he was smelling more into his body.

"Baby if you keep this up, this won't last as long as I'd like for it to. Is this really what you want? Right now?" He had captured her wandering hands and kissed them both before placing them on his chest. "Here for now. Touch me here." Pulling her closer to him, he kissed her.

This kiss wasn't like the others they'd shared. This one felt more possessive, hungrier. He demanded entrance this time, his tongue sliding along her lips and pushing inside when she opened to him. He moaned deeply. She felt it rumble along her body from his. He pressed her back against the mattress and covered her body with his heavy weight.

His hand moved down her ribs and then along her ass, pulling her hard and up into him. She didn't remember getting naked, but they both were. Their skin-to-skin contact was like having the sun beating down on her from high above. She could feel the hardness of his cock through the blanket and slid her leg up his to hook around him, but she wasn't able to because of the stupid blankets that had wrapped themselves between them and mostly around her.

"Christ, I want you. You're hot, and I can smell you, your arousal. I need to taste you, now. I need to taste your sweet cum when you come for me." He began to move down her body, licking and nipping at her as he went. Getting her untangled by the blankets as he went. By the time he had settled himself between her legs, she was wild with a need of her own.

Kaida knew that if he touched her, she was going to come apart. A breath of air over her pussy would have her screaming out loudly her release. And she found that she didn't care either. If he came or not, she was going to come as hard as she could and be damned the consequences of her actions.

She leaned up on her elbows as he sat on his knees. His cock was hard and sticking straight out from his groin. As she watched him, he wrapped his hand around the shaft and pumped his hand up and down. A drop of cum seeped from the tip. Kaida licked her lips, a need to take him into her mouth, making her hungry and aggressive. She started forward, reaching for him, and he stopped her.

"No. Not yet. I would like nothing better than to have you wrap your mouth around me, but I want to taste you more. Next time, I promise you'll be able to do what you want, but next time. Oh love, you're wet, so wet I can see the dampness on your curls." He let go of his cock and touched her pussy with his long slim finger. As much as she wanted to roll her eyes in the back of her head, she knew instinctively that he wasn't finished.

His finger moved slowly along her nether lips, up and down like he had his cock. Her body responded, and she felt her pussy weep more. He hadn't touched her yet, not touched her where she needed. When his finger slowly entered her heat, she opened her legs wider and raised her hips up to meet him.

"Please, Tucker. I want you. I…there's a need, something…I don't… you have to fill it for me please, fill me." Her hips moved up and down with his finger, and when he inserted another into her, she nearly came up off the bed. Whimpering now, she moved faster with his fingers inside of her. For every downward stroke, she was right there meeting him. Christ, this was more than she thought she could handle, more than one man had ever given her before.

"I need to stretch you, love. You're too tight to take me inside of you yet. As much as I'd like to plunder you, I don't want to hurt you either. That's what you want, me to fill you with my cock, isn't it?" He was moving faster now; her body was on fire. "Tell me what it is you wish, little dragon. Tell me what you want, and I'll give it to you."

"Yes, oh yes, please. Make me come, Tucker. Help me over the edge before I fall over it without you there with me." She felt rather than saw him move, her body straining to get to something. When she felt his breath on her thigh, she started to clamp her legs closed, but he held them open with his hands. She was panting now, her need making her ach for release.

With his fingers, he opened her lips and ran his tongue inside her, lapping at her, tasting her. When his mouth closed over her clit and suckled into his mouth, she screamed out her climax, but he didn't stop. While his fingers fucked her, his mouth teased and nipped at her until she came again and again.

"Please, Tucker, please. I want you. I want to suck your cock. Now I want you to come in my mouth." As she reached for him, pulling away from his very talented tongue, she pushed him back against the footboard. She leaned forward and stroked the length of him with just the tips of her fingers. His hiss made her bolder.

"Take me, love. Take me in your mouth. I want to fuck your hot mouth and shoot cum deep into your throat." She was nodding even though she'd never done anything like this before. Had sex, but this wasn't just sex. It was everything in her life that was good rolled into one big event, and tasting Tucker was the gift that she'd never had before.

She swiped her tongue across the tip of the large, deep purple head, taking the cream into her mouth. He hissed again. Bolder than she had ever been in her life, she wrapped her lips around him and licked again. She loved the way he responded. He pumped into her. She didn't know what she was doing, but taking her cues from him and his body, she licked and nipped every inch of him, up one side of his thick vein, then down the other. When she felt his hand touch the back of her head, she felt him guide her, show her what he needed. Soon he was pumping into her hard, his cock bumping the back of her throat again and again.

"I'm going to come, Kaida. Fuck, I'm coming!" Seconds later, she felt the first hot explosion hitting the back of her throat. He pumped harder into her, pulsing into her over and over. She swallowed him, his cum; loving the salty taste that she knew was unique to him. He lifted her up and turned her over onto her hands and knees. She was ready, she thought, so ready for his cock to be deep inside of her. Moaning, she moved back against him.

The sudden intrusion hurt, but as soon as he moved again, she was wanting more. His cock touched parts of her that she'd never felt before. And when he leaned over her, still fucking her hard, she cupped her breast into her hand and licked the hard tip. The roaring sound got louder and louder as he fucked her while holding the other breast in his hands.

Feeling him come like she did caused her to come over and over. Her body was spent, her arms and legs weak. When Tucker dropped atop of her, unable to hold up his weight, she fell forward on the bed and lay there. Even if the house were under threat of a tornado, she would simply die with a huge smile on her face and her naked body for all to see.

Waking up enough to feel that she was being moved, she wrapped her arms around

Tucker, asking him weakly not to drop her. Settling her in the bed, she rolled to her side and let him curl into her body from behind. Kaida really didn't care what happened next. She was so relaxed that she doubted that she would wake up once in the middle of the night to go to the bathroom. She was finished.

She did wake when a ringing noise bothered her. Tucker said that he had it, and she didn't care if it was for her or not. The thought of having a conversation with someone was going to be impossible, and while she would love to know who he was talking to, she really didn't either. Closing her eyes once again, she was fast asleep.

Getting up to go to the bathroom her feet were even sore. Washing her hands when she was finished, all she could think about was her bed. It occurred to her that Tucker was missing from the bed, but she figured that if it was something he needed her for, he knew how to get in touch with her. As soon as she was back in bed, she closed her eyes and let sleep take her under once more.

Waking up, she felt pain. There was no pinpointing it for herself as it was all over her body. It felt like someone was using a yard roller over her, and instead of spikes, it was needles less than an inch apart. Crying out, she felt someone touching her, but the pain was too much for her to see who it was. Just as she was thinking that she couldn't take another roll over her, she fainted.

It didn't feel any better when she was awakened by pain again. Her body was being turned inside out, squeezed, then stretched to the limits of even her own skin would allow it. In all that time, over and over, it hurt her. She could see flashes of things. Dragons and men. Some she knew, others she did not. As she was being twisted up and wrung out, she remembered throwing up at some point and feeling all the pains starting over.

"Kaida? Wake up, honey." She opened one eye and closed it quickly. Telling Tucker that the sun was too bright, she heard the curtains shut and him sit back on the bed. "Are you awake this time? Come on, honey, it's been four days, and I need for you to wake up and talk to me. Please? We all miss you."

"Did you say four days?" when he didn't answer, she looked at him. "Four days? I didn't—what happened to me? Why did I feel like I'd been smushed up and remade?" He grinned at her.

Chapter 6

While she couldn't shift, she had all the powers of a dragon. And then some, even Kingston was impressed with all that she could do. And to her, it was a great deal more than she ever thought that she imagined in her life. She looked over at Tucker when he said her name. When he smiled at her, it was all she could do not to leap at him and take him to the ground. Or any surface that was strong enough to hold them.

"You have to keep practicing on how to blow flames before you set fire to yourself." She pouted. It had been fun heating up a pot of water for tea. But then the heat got away from her, and she had not just boiled out all the water but she'd melted the container so badly that it had to be tossed away. They teased her about that for about ten minutes. At least until she threatened to do the same to them. Kingston joined them in the backyard. It wasn't safe for her to practice in the house. He sat down heavily on one of the patio chairs and looked about as dejected as she'd ever seen him. She asked him what had happened.

"My parents are peppering me about how much money I have. Did I tell you that I purchased the homes surrounding theirs? Well, they are saying that whoever bought the property has been making things look good, and they want to be able to do the same. And as their child, I should want them to have the best because I have the money. I can't wait until they find out that I purchased the houses. That will really burn their toast." Tucker asked him what he was going to do about them. "Nothing. They've been told what happened to Margo. She told Cassian and Brenin that there had been money from their parents will that they could collect on. I'm helping them get it. I don't know if I could have done what they did to her."

"I wasn't aware that they did anything to her? What's happened?" Tucker explained that it had happened while she'd been resting. "Well? Tell me? First, tell me that the two of them are all right. I only meant for them to get some payback from her. Did she hurt them?"

"After she told them about the money and the will that their parents had left, they felt like they were doing her wrong. Not that they didn't enjoy themselves while they had her around." Kaida cocked her brow at Kingston. "Right. What happened to her. They gave her the option of going to prison for the murder of not just their parents but those of Savage—Tucker's as well. She is the reason that you can't kill blood relatives. They couldn't find any evidence of their deaths, but she confessed when she told the council that she wanted to be put to death. It was that or hang out with her brothers for all of eternity."

"Did you know that, Tucker?" He said that he'd known that his parents had been poisoned but never by who. "Well, I don't know whether to be happy about her death or not then. I mean, do you think that you could have reconciled with your family?"

"I don't know that I would have tried to be honest. They left me, not that I left them when they took my sister to all those competition things. They didn't have time for me." He shrugged. "I have always thought that if they had known that I was going to get their money, they would have made it so that it went to some charity or something. Being their only living child, I got everything they had. Honestly? I don't think of them all that often. It's been centuries since I was born and only a few decades less since they've been dead."

She sat down with Kingston. "What do you want to do with your parents? I know that they've been asking for money or demanding it, I mean. What can we do to help you shed them from your life once and for all?"

"I want them out of my life. They're going to keep at me until I give in and then they'll go away only to come around again. I know that it would be easier to just pay them off, but what am I getting out of this? Nothing but a few decades of peace and quiet, the reason that we came here in the first place. I don't want to pay them off but it's the only way that I can see that will get rid of them. They're wearing me down." She asked if he wanted her to take care of them. "I'm almost afraid to let you do that. I know you will, but I'm afraid that you'll get hurt, and that will be the end of me."

"What if I promise you that I'll make it quick if they push me too far?" Kingston asked her if she thought that she could kill them. "I don't know why, but I do. I feel like I can take on the world and make it dance for me. Your parents have done enough to you, and it's time that they paid for it. Or I can go the other way, like Cassian and Brenin did, and offer them a choice. Which do you think they'll choose?"

"I think they'll laugh in your face right up until you kill them." He looked at Tucker and then back at her. "What does Tucker have to say about you taking on some very old dragons? I'm sure that he'd not at all happy about you maybe getting hurt." She turned to look at him, too.

"Being newly mated or not, I have learned very quickly that if she wants something to happen, it will. If she says she can do something, she will. In the event that she gets hurt, not dead but hurt, I will retaliate the same way to whoever harms what is mine." He grinned before speaking again. "You might say that I've learned the hard way what she says is truth and I will stand back until she can do no more."

"Smart man, my husband." She glanced down at the ring that had a band that matched his and felt her happiness all over her body. "Let's get this done. Why don't we? That way, I can go home and have more sex with my savage."

"Christ." Kaida laughed when Kingston's cheeks pinked up. The thought of embarrassing a man as old as he was made her giggle, too. Men, she was beginning to discover, were a lot of fun when you didn't have to work for them. Just making Tucker happy made her feel as good as when she would meet her quota at work. Like she was on top of the world.

Kingston called his parents. They had overstayed their welcome at the hotel they'd been in and had to go to Columbus, where they could stay for less money, but it was further away from their son and his money. And that seemed to be all they wanted, too. His money and, of course, for him to bow before them. She thought them a little off but didn't say anything to Kingston. He had enough on his mind as it was.

"They're going to meet me, not us, in the hotel lobby. I didn't tell them that you were coming if that's all right?" Both she and Tucker said it was probably for the best. "They also told me that they were going to eat someplace where I might have to take out a loan to eat at. Whatever floats their boats. I doubt that they'll eat much once they see that the two of you are with me. And before you ask, yes, I want you both there. Tucker knows how they are. They're all kinds of stubborn, too."

"I'm not worried. Are they the type that likes to make a scene?" He said that if it was to embarrass him, then yes, they were all for it. "I just don't understand people anymore. I'm sure that you guys have had a lot more dealings with them, but they're so into things going their way, aren't they? I never noticed that before."

They arrived at the hotel right on time. Taking a limo would put them all in the same car and make it so that they wouldn't have any choice but to ride with them. If they would even get into the car with them. Kaida didn't think they'd give up the opportunity to embarrass Kingston as much as they could, Tucker. And she was going to bring home the fact that his name was Tucker, not Savage, too. She finally had everyone in town calling him that, and she couldn't have been more happy.

Kingston went into the hotel to get his parents, and she looked at Tucker. He looked wonderful in a suit, and she loved the way that his eyes matched the color of not just her dress but his tie as well. The diamond sparkled over them both and made it all the more romantic, with them being stuck in the limo alone.

"Do you think that they'll come with us?" Tucker said they'd go for just the reason she thought so that they could embarrass the lot of them. "Then we'll have to strike first. What is the one thing that you remember about them that was wrong? You know, like they did something in the public that would embarrass them to no end?"

When he smiled at her, she knew that what he had was juicy. When Kingston came back out alone, she thought that the three of them could have a lovely dinner and maybe even invite the other two to join them. It would be like having her family around. Then she saw them coming out of the hotel.

Sofia was dressed from head to toe in black. A somber black that made William and her look like they were attending a funeral rather than a dinner with their son and his friends. She had no doubt that they weren't ever going to be on friendly terms with the elderly couple, but it made her plans for the evening all the more special. It was going to be fun, too.

"I don't know why you two are here." Tucker told her that it was his limo. "It is not. Why must you tell lies all the time, Savage?"

"My name is Tucker Savage. You can call me that or nothing at all." William asked him why he was being so uppity all of a sudden. "How would you know how I act all the time? Since you got here, that's the first time I've seen you since I was being tried for the murder of my family. Oh yes, I remember you being there, egging the council on to have me killed. And all this time, you knew that Margo had done the deed. Even when Cassian and Brenin's family were killed, you said nothing. What does it feel like to be so wronged? I can tell you, it's not a feeling that ever fades away."

"You would bring that up when we're mourning the death of poor Margo. I can't believe that you did that to her." Kaida said she'd done it. "Really? And why should I believe that? You're nothing but a human that should have been murdered before you were born."

"You mean aborted. Well, lucky me I must have better parents than Kingston has. And that would mean you. But I drew first blood with Margo, and that was our deal. When

I turned her over to her brothers, knowing that they'd be kinder to her than she'd ever been to anyone else, I was surprised to find out that she'd spoken to the two of you — or would that be threatened to two of you with death if you didn't bring her along with you on this trip." Sofia huffed. "Also, I don't know if you're aware of this or not, but the parents of Cassian and his brother left them a great deal of money too. They're getting it in the next couple of weeks."

"We'll see about that. Being that we're the last of the true Savages then I think it should come to us. We're the ones that have kept the two of them in line." Tucker laughed, and she turned an evil eye at him. "Your parent should have dropped you so that you were never born. Christ, when I think of how lovely Lillian was and how you turned out. Even going so far as taking a human as a mate. What is the dragon world coming to?"

"A great deal better once you're out of it." She couldn't read minds and not let them know she was doing it. She had Tucker do it and tell her what was on their mind. When he paused for a moment, she looked at him. He smiled but it was tight and didn't reach his eyes.

"Don't eat anything that I don't hand you." She asked if they were going to poison her. *"Yes. At least, that's their plan. I've already warned Kings. He said that he'd not planned on eating anything anyway. I think that I can get on board with that. After we take care of them, the three of us can go out and have all the food we want. After they're gone. Do you have a plan?"*

"I don't, not really. Just to do what the council asked us to do and get them to confess. I think they will. They already think that they're untouchable. Do you suppose they had a hand in killing the other couples with Margo? I wouldn't put it past them." He said that he'd not either. *"They're what gives dragons a bad name if you ask me. Just pure evil."*

She was happy that they'd spoken to the council before coming here. They apparently had been trying to prove a few murders on them for some time now. Helping Margo would be hard to prove unless they confessed to helping her. But she had no doubt that they'd do more than that.

They were pulling up in front of the restaurant when William looked at her. "You think you're so wonderful that you have a bit of magic, don't you?" Kaida told him that she thought it was wonderful to have a man who loved her very much. "He'll tire of you like all the others around. You'll see. You'll have him a couple of human children, and then he'll kick you to the curb. I give it six months. You'll see."

The man's head snapped back, and she didn't know what had happened. Not until she noticed that Kingston was nursing his hand. He had punched his father in the face, and she thought that it had been a long time coming. Looking at her, he took her hand into his and kissed it. Smiling at her, he told her that he had wanted to be her knight in shining armor for a long time.

~*~

Kings, a new nickname that Tucker had given him, watched his parents' every move. When the breadsticks came, he snatched them from the waiter and handed them to Kaida and Tucker after taking one for himself. If she'd not been looking right at his parents, she might well have missed the look of anger on their faces. When asked if they wanted more, Kings told the waiter that would be wonderful and could he please hand it all to him. The man looked confused but complied with the second batch of bread was brought to the table.

"What do you think you're doing?" Kings asked his mom what she meant. "Do you think that I'm incapable of sharing the bread with you and the others?"

"No. I just think that you'd do more than share with us. It's not that I don't think that you're incapable of sharing, but I don't want any poison that you might have on you getting into my or the others' system." Her face paled a great deal and before she could recover, Kings asked her if she'd been the one to poison any of the other Savages with Margo's help. "No answer? Well, that's all right. I know that you killed them off with her help. Or you might well have coned her into thinking it was all her idea so that you could stay out of trouble when she was caught. Believe it or not, I know a great deal more about you than you do me."

"Like what? Something that the little twit told you about? You're going to believe a human over your own parents? I'm ashamed of you." He laughed, drawing the attention of those around him, and Kaida loved it. "Stop that braying right now. You're making a spectacle of yourself."

That made him laugh all the harder. He must have seen a couple of people smiling at him and decided that she didn't care what people thought about him laughing aloud. It was nice to be able to feel good around his parents for a change. She'd bet anything that Kings would laugh the night away at their expense. When the waiter came to take their order, she noticed that neither Kings nor Tucker had ordered anything but the salad bar. She decided that he was going to do the same.

"What are you doing?" Kings asked his father what he meant. "Ordering from the salad bar. Don't you think you'd like a thick steak and a baked potato? That's what I'm having."

"Yes, you go ahead, but I doubt very much that you'd poison an entire restaurant full of people just to get at us. At least that's what I'm hoping." She noticed that his mother was playing with her charm. Apparently, so did Kings. "You keep playing with that mother, and you might get a bit of the poison on yourself."

Her hand moved away from the charm so quickly that she knew that was where it was. Snatching it from her neck and breaking the chain with it, Kaida held it by the chain and looked at the council that suddenly appeared in the room. Not saying a word, the older couple were gone and so was the charm. Whatever it was, she was glad that they did what Tucker had said and ordered nothing but what they could touch themselves.

After they were gone, they reordered what they wanted. The salad bar was nice. Dragons liked a good bit of greens as much as they loved meat, she'd been told. Ordering the largest steaks they had on their menu, Kaida decided that it was as good a time as any to celebrate. Telling the waiter to bring them their best champagne, they toasted their night and enjoyed the rest of the evening, making plans for the rest of their lives.

The other two cousins joined them just as their meal came to them. Ordering for them, she was glad to see that everyone was in better spirits. She knew that she was. When Kings heard from David about his parents' home coming up for sale, he was glad to be able to buy it as well and have it torn down. There were just too many bad memories of the place for him to want to have it renovated into something nice, he told them. Starting from scratch was the best way to go, she thought.

~*~

On the way home, Kings noticed that Kaida was asleep. She'd had a rough few days and he was glad to see that she was getting the rest that she needed. He looked at Tucker when he spoke.

"She's nearly dragon. While she can't shift into one, she can blow flames and other things that I can do. Even some that I couldn't before she changed." He asked him what he could do now. Instead of answering, he put out his hand, and a ball of fire appeared. "Christ, that's amazing. Is there anything else?" Tucker laughed. "I'm sorry, I was just excited."

"That's fine. She can do the same, but her ball is smaller, and she can toss them. Once mine leaves my hand, it's gone. She's been able to change her clothing at will since I met her, but now she can have her hair done up and her heels on. By the way, when you meet your mate, have her wear high heels. Trust me, you'll love it." He felt his heart ache for that. "You'll meet her, Kings. I know it. There is someone out there for all of us. We'll be old dragons with mates that make you feel a thousand years younger. Also, she can speak and read dragon. I'm a little rusty on it but it's coming back to me. It makes it nice when you don't want anyone else to understand what it is you're saying."

"Do you really think there is a mate out there for all of us? I have to tell you, sometimes

I'm jealous of the love between the two of you. And to think you were ready to toss her aside when you first met her." He said he'd been an ass. "That you were. But it turned out all right."

When they arrived home, dropping him off first, he thought about the houses that he'd seen the other day. While he could well afford to buy them all, he just wanted to settle into one home that wasn't as large as the one he was in now. Why did he think that he needed such a big house to begin with was beyond him. But he'd find something, and he'd live happily there without a care in the world.

By the time the sun was coming up, he'd decided on three houses that he wanted to look at. One of them had a pool for which he was happy about, but the kitchen looked out of date. He could easily fix that, but for now, he was happy to have something smaller and one that he could manage. Four bedrooms wasn't all that much but it was something that he could work with.

Calling the realtor that Tucker had used, she set him up with the three that he'd found, as well as two more that weren't on the market just yet. He had explained to her that he wanted to sell the house that he currently had and wondered if she thought it would be on the market very long. The house with a pool had been on the market for nearly seven years before it sold.

"It's a large house, and people with families are looking for more than they can handle nowadays. Like a status symbol. Understand?" He said that he did. "Also, you've kept up on the house. The kitchen is brand new. You said that you put a new roof on it. I would guess that the first day it's on the market, you'll have bids that double what you want for it."

"That sounds really good to me. I don't have a house payment. I only took out a fifteen-year loan. I've lived in it for nearly thirty, so anything that I make over asking will be wonderful." He didn't need the money, but he wasn't going to turn down a good deal because he was stupid. "The furniture can stay or not too. I'm starting fresh."

"I'll come and pick you up, and the two of us can go over what stays and doesn't. I think you're going to be a perfect pick for the house that I have in mind. It has a pool, as you requested, and it's ready to move into. I don't know if you play pool or not but there is a pool table in the basement that you can have friends over with. Also, there is an overly large entertainment area down there, too, complete with wet bar and chairs." She'd pushed all the right buttons, but the yard that he wanted to have. He'd been able to shift in his own yard here, the reason that he'd gotten the big house and was hoping that she'd only skipped over it in favor of the other things on his life. "I'll be there in twenty minutes, Kings."

After walking around his home for two hours, he realized how much he didn't use of the big mansion. There were bedrooms that didn't even have a bed in them, and the kitchen, while up to date, it didn't have any touches that it would have had someone cooked in there all the time. He was glad to be going smaller. Simply because he wanted to know his home rather than have no idea how my bathrooms it had because he'd never ventured from the one in the master suite.

Cassian joined him on the trip to the houses. He said that it occurred to him as well that he didn't want to be in a large place right now. Instead, like he and Tucker had done, he wanted a smaller home that he could keep up with rather than have cobwebs in the rooms that he'd not known anything about.

"It seemed that at the time, going big or going home was our motto. I've discovered that while it was nice for a while, I'm bored with it. And when I date someone, it's all they can see is dollar signs. Not that I don't have a lot of money, but I know better than just handing it out to anyone who comes along with their hands out. I'm sick of that as well." Kings asked him when the last time he'd been on a date. "Years. It's not fun anymore. Getting to know someone before they tell you that you need to help them out or one of their family members. That drives me insane. Mostly, I date shifters when I want to go out. They seem to understand more than most that I'm not into a long-term relationship with them just to get laid once in a while. Even that's become boring, too. One-night stands aren't what I want right now. Especially after seeing Kaida and Tucker together. They sort of hum with happiness."

"I know what you mean. They seem to exude happiness. I'm sort of jealous of them too. And to think that he didn't want anything to do with her. She's made him a better man too. Don't you think?" He agreed with him and then said that he didn't know if there would be that much happiness for him in the future. "Nah, we'll have it. I have to believe that, or I might as well end my life. I need to know that there is something out there for all of us or what's the point?"

"I guess so." Changing the subject, they looked over the first of all the houses. It was all right, he thought but not worth the amount that they were asking for it. When they got to the second house, one that wasn't on the market just yet, he fell in love with it even before going into the place to see what was going to be needed. "Look out back. If you don't buy this place, then I am. It's perfect."

Three bedrooms and three baths were just a little smaller than he had wanted, but Cassian was right. There was enough room to add onto the place without messing up the structure of the house. The pool in the back was nice. Large and well maintained. Even the pool house attached to the boat house made him think that he could enjoy living here alone or with a mate. But it was the house that he fell in love with, too.

It was small, yet it was as the yard was, well maintained. It looked like he could entertain in the kitchen as well as the dining room and not have anyone tripping over one another. He could almost see the addition of extra rooms in the place as there was that much room to do it with. When he entered the dining room, he was ready to make an offer. It was the perfect size for entertaining his family and some room for mates as well. He needed to believe that there was someone out there for him to make this house a home.

The two of them toured the house together. There were things that needed to be done to it to make it livable. The bathrooms needed to have showers in them as he didn't care for baths, though he was keeping one as a tub shower combo in the event that he had little ones around the house. Smiling to himself, he was happy to make an offer on the house without seeing the others. Even if the others were better, he'd be able to rent this one out for the extra income.

By the end of the afternoon, he'd made offers on two of the houses, and Cassian had made one on the house next door to the first one they'd made an offer on. It was nice, he thought, to be so close to his family — excluding his parents — his cousins were all that he needed in the world.

Chapter 7

Kaida walked up and down the street a third time. Something or someone was calling for her, and she didn't understand the freaking magic that was having her walking the street like some kind of idiot. As she passed the restaurant once more, she decided that she was going to eat. Maybe that was all it was. She needed some food, and the magic was telling her to get her ass in gear and eat.

"You couldn't just say that, could you?" Waiting to be seated, she felt this was right. The place was calling to her, and she was going to sit down and have a good meal. As she was being seated, Kaida bumped ever so slightly into the waitress who was coming toward her and nearly fell to the ground when the surge of power washed over her. Sitting down rather than chancing another step, the woman asked her if she was all right. Simply putting her hand onto her arm told her everything she needed to know about the other woman.

"He's coming for you. Today. You're not safe here." The girl looked around before jerking her arm from her. "He's your ex-husband, and he wants your son. I can protect you."

"What are you talking about?" She laughed, but it was strained. "I don't have any children, nor have I ever been married." Pulling her hand to her, she pointed to the marks where a band might have been.

His name is Jason, and your name is Skye. Your last name is Houston, but you changed it to Wilson so that you could find a job. The people here think that your first name is Amanda. Your son's name is Matt. He's ten. Very smart for his age because you've been tutoring him for the last four years." She put her hand on her arm again. "Your parents are both dead, and you believe that Jason killed them. Your son is right now hiding out in an abandoned home so that he can be safe."

"What are you talking about?" Skye

looked around before standing up. "Lady, I don't know where you got your information, but you're wrong. About it all."

"He'll be coming through the door with a gun in about two minutes." Instead of arguing with her more, she took off her apron and headed to the back of the place. Kaida told her to come and sit with her. He'd never see her if she did. "I promise you, Skye, he'll never touch either of you again."

Instead of arguing anymore, she slipped into the empty booth next to them, and Kaida joined her. Almost as soon as she put her arm around her shoulder, the door opened, and just as she said, a man came in with a gun pointed at the place. The small whimper that Skye made had nearly had her jump out of her skin when the man looked in their direction.

Shooting his gun to the ceiling, he asked where she was. He was looking for Skye Houston, and they had better turn her over to him, or he'll kill someone every ten minutes if they don't bring her to him.

"I don't know any Skye Houston." The

manager looked around and then back to the man. "I have staff here by the name of Amanda and Carol Anne. Other than that, I can't help you."

Jason pointed the gun at the man's head, and it was all she could do not to get up and slam her magic into the man and kill him. Instead, she reached out to all the family and begged them to come to her. That she had a problem she was in over her head with. It was Tucker who answered her first and asked her where she was.

After telling them all what was going on she also told them that she was hiding a woman by the name of Skye. Also, that someone needed to go and get her son, or he might well be in trouble as well. It was Kings that said he'd get the boy, at least make sure that he was all right.

She knew that Skye's son would be all right with Kings watching over him, and she was never so happy with anyone as she was to see Tucker and Brenin come into the place next. With a short pop to the back of the head, the man was down, and his gun went flying.

For the silence when the man fell to the floor, there was so much noise that she wanted to clamp her hand over Skye's mouth to shut her up. Instead, all she did was put her hands over hers and tell her to calm down.

"I have to go to Matt." She told her that he was fine. The look she gave her had Kaida thinking that she didn't believe her. "He's all I have in the world. We've been running for the last five years, and I need to keep him safe."

"I understand that. But he's with my cousin-in-law, and he's bringing him here to you. But you have to think for me. What is the code name that you use to know that it's safe to go with him." She told her that it was *April Showers bring May flowers.* "That's a good one. I love it. All right, Kings is bringing him here. Then we'll head to our house and see what we can do about keeping the two of you safe from now on. I'm under the opinion that we just bury him in the back yard someplace there are red ants, but that's just me."

Skye laughed. It was nervous sounding but not nearly as stressed as before. The police arrived and no one mentioned that he was there for Skye. Amanda Wilson would be safe as well as the owner of the place was going to fire her for leaving in the middle of the shift. Kaida was able to get her out of the place without anyone seeing her.

"I need some juice." There was a juice bar not far from where they were, so she and Skye headed there. "I was told that when I use a lot of magic that I was going to need to have more fruit and juices in me." Kaida babbled on while Skye looked around.

She didn't know if she was worried that someone might recognize her or she was looking for her son. But when Kings showed up with him in his car, the reunion was tearful. She was glad now that she didn't ignore the need to get out of the house and walk the streets. Kaida was sure that she had saved the woman, for he would have killed her to get to her son.

After heading back to their home, she got her another glass of juice. She expected Tucker to ask her what she'd been doing but all he did was to ask her if she was all right. She was, she told him, but for being really dry.

He went into the kitchen and brought her back a large pitcher of what looked like orange juice. She nearly drained it in favor of talking. When she was feeling better, she turned and looked at Skye and her son.

"How did you know?" confused for a second, she asked her what she meant. "About him coming to get me. For all I know, you told him where I was, and when he brought in the — don't answer that. I'm sorry. You wouldn't have risked your life if that had been the issue. But I would like to know how you did that."

"What do you know about the Savage family?" She said that it was reported that they were shifters, dragons of all things. "They're both. Shifters and dragons. I'm mated to Tucker, now married, and with that, I was able to get some of his magic and a bit of my own. When asked by the council, they said that I must have had a dragon sometime in my family and that's why I can do as much if not a few extra things that Tucker can't do. You needing help from me called to me while I was home, and I came to figure it out."

She went on to tell her how she was ready to give up and get some lunch when she bumped into her. Telling her what she got from that small touch. It was Tucker that finished up for her.

"My little dragon called for help, and we came to help her. I've seen Mr. Houston in—" she told them that she'd never been married to Jason, but he'd asked her out, and things went downhill from there. "I'm sorry then. Is Matt his son?"

"No. He's not really mine, either. I was on the run, and so was he. But someone put a flyer out for a million dollars if they were to bring Matt back to them. He said that he didn't know where they were going to get that much money as they always told him that they were broke." She looked at the young man, and when he nodded, she continued. "They do have money. A great deal of it. But they only brought Matt around when they had people over for dinner and such. He's very brilliant and can read something once, and he knows it word for word. Other things as well, but he didn't want to be their...he called it a dog and pony show anymore, so he ran away about the same time that I did, and we just clicked."

When dinner was served, the two of them looked as if they were going to sob. Apparently, it was the first hot meal they'd had since getting together and on the run. Even the meal that she got at work, she'd bring it back to the house and share it with him.

After dinner, Tucker made a few calls. They were going to be safe in their home. As soon as she showed them their rooms, she was sure that they could have slept standing up. Since she had no idea how to give magic to someone, Kaida asked Tucker to give them the magic of clothing. Skye said it had been several days since she'd been able to get to the laundromat, and she needed some clean clothing on her back. Everywhere else, she told her too.

She was nearly ready for bed, too, when Matt came to find them. He said that he wanted to talk to them since they'd been so kind as to help him out of the situation that they'd been in.

"My parents are Matthew and Delilah Connor. I'm sure that you've heard of them. They have heard of you." Tucker said that he'd had a few dealings with them, too. "I thought so. They don't have a very high opinion of you and your cousins. You're not old money like they are. I'm not sure where they got that, as I'm sure you're older than this town, but they think that you shouldn't be allowed in respectable places because of how you got your money. How did you get your money?"

"As you guessed, we've been around forever. Made investments in things that were new then but still around today. Like lumber companies. Computers and phones. You might as well know that we've been the start-up for a lot of things that are going on in his world today. One of them being airplanes." Matt said that he knows about investments as well, and that was what had saved his parents from ruin. "However, I stopped doing that as well when I got smart enough to know that they didn't care if the company was selling shares or not. They were going to invest in it."

"I've heard about that as well. They're being looked at for a couple of murders, too. I wouldn't put it past time to kill, but I don't know them all that well." Matt said that he did and knew that they had done that and more. "I would imagine."

Matt told them of a few other things that he could do as well. "My father figured out that I could see a bit into the future when it came to investments. As far as I know, he never said anything to my mother, but he would beat me regularly when I didn't give him what he wanted. What he never figured out was that not only can I see the futures on a lot of the things they wish to invest in, I can see the ones that fail after a few years too. Those are the only ones that I would give him. As you can well imagine, they didn't appreciate that too much."

"So this man, Jason, he's been looking for you and he just so happened to be looking for Skye as well." Kaida snorted and asked for the real truth as to why she was with him. "I saved her a couple of times. She knows I have some abilities. Whenever Jason gets too close, I can tell her. I messed up this time because I wasn't paying attention to the signs that were given to me. He figured out that she was with me and then that I was the boy who was worth a million dollars. He told me once that he was killing two birds with one pistol. Jason isn't very bright and has a one-track mind. Also, he bets on the ponies, and that is why he's desperate for the money he'll get for turning me in."

Kaida was beginning to see other things too that the boy could do. He'd brought a Danish to himself at dinner. Also, his napkin that had fallen in the gravy on his plate was once again clean when he gave it a hard shake. Little things that she had to wonder if the kid even knew he was doing. Looking at him now, she wondered, too, if he realized that he could hide from his family without much in the way of thought.

"I know that." She asked him what he meant. "That I can hide myself away. I could have easily taken all their money, too, but I have to protect Skye. She's the only person that I know who has never expected anything from me other than her friendship. Not to mention, she's been kinder to me than anyone I've ever encountered other than you guys."

"Thank you, young man. You've no idea how much we appreciate that." He nodded and then looked around the room. "What are you looking for. You've been looking around this place since you arrived."

"There are secrets in the walls here that you could get to. Some of its money and jewels, but there is not just a journal tucked away but an old bible as well." Tucker asked him if he knew where it was. "I do. It's just above the fireplace and near the pocket doors. I know you have no use for the money that you find, but I have a feeling that the people you brought this house from could use it."

"I'll do that." Matt showed him where each piece of history was hidden. In addition to the things that he'd told them about, there was a bundle of silverware, several more diaries, as well as the first deed to this place that had been built by the family on the original fifty acers. "Are there any pictures of this place?"

"Plenty that have been hidden away as well. There is an old barn out back that you might want to go through as well. You'd be surprised at how much one family can horde away when they don't want anyone to take it from them. The original name for this place was called Manchester Manor. When you make the improvements on this place, the extra three bedrooms and baths, you'll find a hidden room that is also full of things that were stashed away during the wars."

They'd only just spoken of adding other rooms to the place this morning. It thrilled her that she'd be able to find a bit of history about the place and perhaps put some of the pictures on display around the rooms. She was especially happy to find the old money. She'd frame it up and hang it on the walls as well.

After Matt left them, they headed up to

bed as well. Almost too excited to sleep, she curled herself about Tucker's warmth. In the morning, they were going to have to figure out what to do about Matt's parents as well as the man looking for Skye. He needed to be dealt with by one of the dragons she thought.

Kaida wondered if Skye was mated to any of the cousins. She was disappointed when she realized that they'd all been around her, and no one had said a thing. Maybe they were just supposed to help her. She could do that, too. Help someone who was as down on their luck as she'd been before getting with this family.

Sure, she had a bit of money in the bank but now she had so much more than currency. She had a love of her life, a home, not a house as well as magic that she could use to help others. Kaida thought that she could help others all the time if it was as easy as it had been with Skye and Matt. She also knew that this was a rare case and that she wasn't going to have it as easy as she did today. Things just clicked for the two of them.

~*~

Tucker decided that they needed a bigger bed, this one was all right but when Kaida tried to pull away from his heat, she was nearly off the bed. Holding her was wonderful, but he didn't want her to suffer needlessly if he could do something about it.

When she rolled over atop of him, taking his body to the mattress, he held her to him and watched her face. There was little to make him think that she was exhausted anymore but needed him. And Christ, he needed her with every breath he took.

This woman, above all others, made him feel things he'd never felt before. His need for her never ceased to amaze him. His mouth crushed against her, and he took whatever she had to offer. It seemed to him that she was offering her all to him. His dragon was happy with the turn of events as well.

Her body responded to his need immediately. Sitting up, he lifted her up so that her soft folds met intimately with his hard cock. As soon as Kaida wrapped her legs around his hips, he took them to the floor. Neither of them was hurt, but the harder surface was much nicer than the slightly too soft bed. Pulling away from her, he was on his knees between her legs on either side of him.

He rested back on his heels while he looked down at her. "Take off your jammies, Kaida. I need you. I want to fuck you right now."

While she pulled her top from her bottoms and unbuttoned it, he worked at the snap and zipper of her pants that he'd yet had no time to disrobe for her. Standing to pull them off her, he stripped off his own shirt and tossed it behind him. The sight of her in only her bra and panties made his cock jerk hard in his pants.

"Take off your bra. Make your nipples hard for me, baby. Make them ache for me." He felt his teeth drop in anticipation of tasting her. His dragon wanted a bit of her as well. He loved her taste, her scent that she exuded just for him. When his eyes began to turn, her body was outlined in a deep red that made his need sharp. Stripping his pants off with his boxer briefs, he stood before her naked and stroked his cock while she watched, her nipples beading hard as she rolled and squeezed them for him.

"Tucker, please. I need you. I want to feel you inside of me. I want you to drink from me, you and your dragon. Make me come hard. Please, baby. I want to feel you come deep inside of me." His low growl had her eyes roll to the back of her head.

Tucker knew he wouldn't last if she touched him now. He needed to take the edge off, needed to sip from her so that he would last longer than it would take for him to enter her. Dropping back down, he ran his hands up her thighs and his fingers under her tiny thong. Gripping it in his hands, he looked into her eyes, and he tore it from her body. Her cry of hunger made the teeth from his dragon burst more through his gums.

"I'm dying here, Kaida. I need to take you quickly. Fast, hard, and dirty. Roll over for me. I need you too much to do this any other way."

When she rolled to her belly and curved

her body up over her knees, he growled at her. Her arousal was strong, and he could see her pussy was wet. Pushing her head down to the floor, he nudged his cock at her entrance.

She coated him with her juices. Grabbing her hips and pulling her hard back against him, he slammed into her hard and deep. Her answering groan nearly sent him over the edge. Pulling out to nearly the tip and slamming again, he felt her grip around him; her tight sheath wrapped around him tightly and sucked him deeper. He felt his climax grip his balls, and the tingle of it run up his spine. Reaching his hand around her front and finding her clit, he pulled hard on it and then squeezed. Over and over, he tormented it until she started to grip him tighter.

"Tucker, now! Please, I'm coming now. Take me." Leaning forward, he licked at her shoulder and then sank his sharp teeth deep into her. The hot, spicy blood filled his mouth as she came, milking him and bringing him over the edge with her. As he filled her with his seed, she took him deeper inside of her. Sealing the bite marks with his tongue, he pulled her up so that both of them were on their knees, and he was still buried deep inside of her. Tucker pressed his wrist to her mouth and moved slowly inside of her again as she bit into him and drank, bringing her to another climax. As soon as she sealed the wound with her saliva, he tilted her back and took her throat. If this didn't change her into his little dragon, he was sure that there wasn't any other way to do it. He had to try. She was his all, his everything to him and his dragon.

Taking enough to make his dragon happy, too, he licked her throat and kissed the large wound. He held her to his body, feeling her heartbeat return to normal and her breathing slow. He wanted her again, but not now. He would move them to the bed soon.

"Tucker, I love you very much. I don't know what I would have done without you all these months when you found me. You've made me so very happy."

"And you me, my love. You have given me a reason to live and a reason to smile.

Let's get to bed so that I can make love to you properly."

Lifting her gently in his arms, he carried her to the bed and snuggled in behind her. Holding her to his body, he felt when she relaxed against him. Smiling he was warmed by her security of being next to him.

Getting up to clean up, he looked in the mirror and wondered not for the first time how he'd been so lucky to have her in his life. He'd been a royal prick when he'd met her, and he was happy for the changes that she'd made in him when she'd told him how much she loved him. Every time she said that he was more in love with her than he'd been before.

He was nearly down the stairs when he thought about his cousins. He only wanted the best for them but doubted that they might find a love like he did. They were jealous, he knew, but Tucker also knew that if any of them could make it work, it would be the others. They were much smarter than he was by a great measure.

With his computer turned on, he decided to take some chances with some of the investments that Matt had told him about. When that was finished, he looked up the Connors to see what sort of people they were. The first thing that appeared was their missing son and how much reward they were offering for his safe return. He wondered what they'd do if they knew that he wasn't going to be going home with them again, as far as he was concerned. The kid had taken a piece of his heart, and he didn't know if he could let him go back to the family that had treated him so wrongly.

"Are you up?" He told Kings that he was. *"Are you alone, too?"* He told him again that he was. *"Good. I have something that I need to talk to you about, and I don't want you to mention it to Kaida. She's scary when she thinks that she is right about something. How did you know that Kaida was your mate?"*

"I got an overwhelming feeling of protection toward her. She knew first, too, I think. But it was more than just a little protection. I felt as if something were to happen to her, I'd die, and I just couldn't let her hurt. Seeing her — Is Skye your

mate?" He told him that he didn't know, but the boy needed his protection, and he thought he'd die if anything were to happen to either of them. *"They told us tonight that they're not related. They just happened to be on the run at the same time."* There was more to it than that, but he knew that it wasn't his story to tell.

"Then I might be wrong. When I went to find the boy, it was all I could do not to grab him up in a huge hug and tell him how much he meant to me. I got the same from the woman, but not like I needed to protect her, but that she would and could protect Matt and me both. Am I making any sense?" He told him that he was. It was just what he felt about Kaida when she found him. *"But for the boy? I don't think so. He's too young, and I'm not into children. No, I'm wrong, and that's the way it should be."*

They talked for a few minutes more as he worked on the investments. Tucker was also able to find a reputable firm to tell him about the things that they'd be finding. He'd, of course, ask Matt about the firm, and that was all right as well.

"*Are we still going to go over the projects that we have going? I have a feeling that between the five of us, we can make a huge difference in a few people's lives.*" He told Kings how much Kaida was looking forward to it as well. "*Also, the computer projects are coming along nicely. They were able to get enough donations that they could buy four computers with printers and I said we'd purchase another four so that they'd have enough to put into the library. I was surprised that they wanted to go with that. I expected them to demand that we bought six more so they'd have the ten that they originally wanted.*"

After making arrangements to get the computers taken to the library, they closed the connections. After investing in the ten places that Matt had told him to, he looked up more about the boy. There was never any mention of him being brilliant but there was an article about his parents trying to get him into college at ten. The boy had played dumb, and that had pissed them off so much that they sent him away to military school, where he was able to escape.

For a kid, he had a good head on his shoulders and was glad that he'd shared his secret with all of them. He hoped that Kings was wrong about Skye and that she was indeed his mate. Or one of the others? He didn't care so long as the boy was around to hang out with. He was easy to speak to and to have an intelligent conversation with.

Making his way back up to the bed, he realized how exhausted he was. He and Kaida had been making love every day and night, and while he knew that it was wearing him down, he couldn't imagine what it was doing to her. He was going to have to make her behave herself and perhaps wear a sack over her body. But then he realized that it would do little good. He knew just what she looked like in anything she wore. Smiling when she curled around him again, he tossed the blankets off of the two of them because he knew that his dragon would keep them both warm. Besides this way he could look at her longingly without her jumping his bones again. And again.

Chapter 8

"How long will you be gone?" Kings was packing his things as he spoke to them. He told her that he'd be gone for about two weeks but would have all the investments that they have taken care of. "Taken care of how? And why can't you do that from here?"

"I've been doing it from here. And it's not getting done. I have to go there and face to face with them so that our money is where it belongs. It's millions of dollars that are tangled up in a weave of lies, and if I don't go now, we may never get it back." She asked him if he needed to go alone. "No. But my cousins are busy. I'd take you with me, but I think that Tucker would have a cow."

He would too. They were having so much fun being a married couple that she couldn't stand for him to be much more than an arm's length away from her before she missed him terribly. Not even explaining to her that they had lifetimes together could she get over the fact that he was going to leave her someplace. That had come from Kings' parents. His father had said it would only last six months before he'd drop her to the curb. Kaida was very insecure like that.

Taking him to the airport, she felt like she was losing a part of herself. The man was only going to be gone for a couple of weeks, and she was being silly. On the way home, she tried to console herself with thoughts of the party when he returned, but that wasn't working either. She missed him too much. It wasn't as if they didn't have a lot to do while he was gone.

"Matt's parents arrived in town this morning. They're staying at the hotel just outside of town. It's a nice little place, much nicer since it was renovated some years ago." She asked Tucker what the plan was for them. "Nothing yet. It's not like we can keep their son from them. Just keep hiding him away so that they don't do a snatch-and-grab with him. I shudder to think what it is they'd do to him when they find him. They'll more than likely put him under lock and key, and that would be bad for him."

"What about that guy, Jason? What can we do about him?" Tucker told her that he was in jail and would be for a while yet. "I guess opening fire in a restaurant full of people will get your ass in trouble in more ways than one."

"He didn't have any kind of permit to carry either. Not to mention him being a convicted felon who had a gun specification on his record." They stopped just outside of town to pick up some things for dinner. They were having fun feeding Matt. He had the appetite of a full-grown man and the silliness of a child. Plus, he was very intelligent, too.

Thanks to Matt, they knew what his parents looked like. So when they stepped out of the grocery store with a photo in their hand, Tucker stepped back so they'd not have to encounter them. They looked pinched in the face, plus years older than she thought that they would with a child of Matt's age. She was going to look into that as well.

Keeping an eye on the couple in the parking lot, the two of them picked up the things to make your own Sundays for dessert tonight. They were also having pizzas as it was the cook's night off. She was going to make things for a cookout, but it was Skye who wanted hot pizza right out of the oven, and who could turn that down.

"Excuse me." She turned when someone spoke behind her, and she smiled at the couple. Up close, they looked beaten, like not having their son around was making them lose some grip on their livelihood. Taking the picture when it was shoved at her, she looked at the picture of Matt. It was an old picture taken when he was about seven or so. "Have you seen our grandson?"

She nearly let the cat out of the bag when she nearly asked if he was her son or grandson. Looking at the picture, she could see too that Matt didn't look a bit like his parents, not even an eye color that would maybe make it so that they looked related.

"I don't remember anyone like that. I

think that I would too if a child that little was all by himself." She explained that he was ten now and not necessarily hanging out alone. "Oh, so he's with his mother or something? Not that it matters. I've never seen him before."

"Why would you say that?" The woman's voice was sharp and mean. Taking a step back, she told her that she'd not meant anything by it. Only making an observation. "You think that I'm too old to have a son this age? Well, I'm sick of people assuming anything when it comes to him. He's my son, not my grandson, and I don't want to hear another word from you."

They had drawn a crowd now, and she hated that. When Mr. Moore, the store manager, asked her if she was all right, she told him that she was but that the woman seemed out of sorts. As her husband — whoever he was — started pulling her along, Kaida could hear him telling her to hush up before the police were called.

"They've been all over town about three times whipping out that picture and asking people if they've seen him. I've told her at least a dozen times that I've never seen him. But that doesn't stop her. She's also looking for a woman and a man. I don't know what to think about that but if you were to ask me, it seems sort of fishy. They're a might too old to be his parents, then all of a sudden today they are his grandparents. What's this world coming to, Mr. Savage?" Mr. Moore shook his head in disgust. Tucker said that he didn't know but would look into it if necessary. "You go on and do that for us. She's being a pain in the ass, pardon my speech, but just look at them every day—I'd probably be doing the same thing if it was my boy. I know that, but why don't they move on? We've done told them that we've never seen him. Now, this man and woman are someone they're searching for."

"Could it be the same man that shot up Travelers the other day?" It was funny that she was just going to say that when one of the others said it first. "I heard he was looking for a boy too. You think those people are out to kidnap all our kids? Well, they come around my house, and I'll show them how we greet the door in his town. I'll blow them away."

"Mr. Jacobs, you don't want to be killing anyone. It might be all the stress of losing their son or grandson. I don't know which." No one seemed to have any idea what their names were either. Kaida thought that odd. To be showing off a picture without any means of contacting them if they were to see the boy. She wanted to race home now and tell Matt what they had discovered but they needed to be calm about this. Calm and collected until they had more news.

After getting their things bagged up, they headed out the door. Having pizzas tonight seemed slightly spoiled because of the people around town. But she'd bet anything that if Matt were to walk down the main street right now, no one would tell the Connors. She was going to ask him about his grandparents, too.

"I've lived with them all my life, and they told me that I was their son. It never occurred to me that they might be my grandparents until just now." He handed back her phone with a confused look on his face. "How would we find out if they are my parents or not? I mean, not that I ever looked for one, but I never saw a birth certificate when I was living with them."

After getting his birth date and social security number, Brenin started to do a search on him. Coming up with the name of the hospital became something of a trial, as he couldn't remember anyone mentioning that. After about two hours of searching and making pizzas, they had little more information than when they started. Just the name of the hospital that he might have been born in and a record of his social being used about fifty years before he'd been born. It was making more questions than answers, she thought.

"I have a plan." Cassian said he wasn't going to tell anyone his plan in the event that it didn't work. She was all right with that, and so was everyone else. About an hour after they'd exhausted every little bit they could find out, one of the members from the local pack came to the house with a bunch of pictures. She worked in the hotel and was a cleaning lady for them.

Getting the information hadn't been all that difficult. All she'd had to have done was go in like she was cleaning, finding the paperwork, and taking pictures. After tidying up the room, she left and finished out her shift. Kaida thought that it was just too easy to get the information from the room and decided that she was going to use the safe in the rooms when she had something to hide.

"I have DNA, too, that I found in the bathroom. The mister must be a diabetic, and when he pricks his finger, it leaves me enough blood to get some information from that." Kaida shivered, thinking of all the things that were left behind when people stayed at hotels. "I have a friend that I'm sending this off to, and when we get the results back, we'll have a better understanding."

Beth was able to take Matt's DNA, too, and that was sent off as well. Once they got the results back, in a couple of weeks, they were told, then they could work from there. At least they'd know how or even if he was related to the elderly couple at all.

In addition to the things that she located, there were things in the room that had startled her. There were handcuffs as well as chloroform. A body bag, too, that was still in the package. All she could think about now was that she was thrilled that she'd never given them any information when she'd seen them today or the other day. These people weren't right in the head and she was slightly afraid of what they might do in order to get Matt back to them.

"There is no record of birth filed in the county that he was born in. There are no files with the Connors name on them either. No homes, no driver's license. They have never voted either, as far as I can tell. I can't find a place where they have voted or even registered to vote with their registration on it." She asked what that meant. "They aren't real. At least as far as the county is concerned."

The more they dug, the deeper they were in with questions. If he was their child, there should have been something that would have had his name on it. There wasn't anything. The car that they drove around was a rental but it wasn't registered to anyone they could find. Just a post office box number that didn't exist either.

Digging into Jason's life. They found more information on him than she could have imagined. He had convictions all up both his arms. Armed Robbery, solicitation, hit and run, as well as kidnapping. That was all there was in the top few of the list and she sat down at the table.

"How does he keep getting out of jail? It looks to me like he's been let out at least a dozen times after only serving a few weeks. Who is releasing him? And why?" No one had an answer and she knew that they wouldn't. "It's too bad we don't know anyone with... maybe I can do it."

"Maybe you can do what?" She explained to them how she needed to find Skye and that she'd only had to touch her before she was able to not just figure out who she was but also that she needed her help. "It's worth a shot. What do you need?"

"I'm not sure. Let me just think about

this for a minute." She sat down with all the paperwork that they had on the man and the older couple and started touching things. She could get little bits of information on them but nothing more. When she picked up the DNA package, she felt a swarm of information roll over her until she had to let it go. She looked up at Tucker.

"It's bad, isn't it?" She nodded, and he sat down beside her. "All right. Tell me, and we'll work from there. Or you tell me what I need to do, and I'll do it. I trust you with my life, love, and we can do this together."

Almost as soon as he touched her with his hand, she knew that he was getting all the information that she'd found. Even Matt's real name and that of the people that he'd been born to.

"They killed them. Like they were nothing, they killed his parents to get to the boy when they found out about how smart he was and what he could do." She nodded and waited for him to continue. "They killed that young couple just because they had a smart son, and they wanted him for his magic."

"Not just that. They wanted his inheritance. However, they were never able to collect on it due to the fact that they'd have to admit who Trevor—his real name, was and how he'd come to be with him. Greed and evilness. If that wasn't enough, they stole all the things that he had at his house and took it with them. Wiping out all evidence of the boy even being there. The couple is buried under their home so that they could keep a good eye on them never being found."

"Christ." Tucker got up to pace. He was tossing out comments like he was giving this a great deal of thought and tossing them away nearly in the same breath. He was pissed, she could tell that, and worst of all, she didn't know how they could make the Connors pay for what they'd done. "He was only one, so it stands to reason that he'd probably not remember his own parents. Or he does and that's what is keeping him up at night. I know he has nightmares. I hear him crying out when he goes to sleep."

"We have to do something. I don't know that much about laws to know where to even begin." He said that he might well know someone. "Good. But before we do anything, we're going to have to tell Skye and Trevor what we figured out. And how. It's the least we can do to keep them safe if they know what they're up against."

"I agree." He continued to pace the room and when he stood in front of her again, she knew that he'd hit on something but wasn't very happy with it. "If she were a mate to one of my cousins, this would be so much better for her. But they all said that they didn't think she was and—"

"Didn't *think* she was?" He nodded, then smiled. "So there is a chance like you didn't know that she's someone's mate, and they just don't know how to figure it out. Christ, Tucker, if I could find your parents right now, I'd dig them up and kill them again. Who treats their children like they did and think that it's all right?"

"Not just my parents but all of our parents.

I think they were sick with money and power, and it went to their head." She agreed with him. "There are a couple of things that I can take care of right now, but in the meantime, you do your thing with whomever you thought could help. Tonight, we'll sit down with Trevor and Skye and tell them what we've figured out. Maybe they'll have some more information once we start telling them what we've figured out."

He kissed her on her mouth and left her there. She wondered if there would ever be a time when she didn't want him to leave her. Things were heating up concerning the young man and his guardian. She only hoped that she could keep them safe until such time that they could figure out if they were mates or not with one of the others.

She liked Skye and hoped that they could be long-lasting friends. If only they could get the things cleared up with the couple and Jason. They were going to have to go and soon. Kaida didn't even care if the lot of them were killed or put into prison, so long as they were out of their lives.

~*~

Skye wasn't sure if what they were telling her was the truth of things but she also had no reason to not believe them. To think that the boy she'd been taking care of for the last few years wasn't even their son nor grandson, and he had magic, too. She wondered for a moment if she had been caring for him or if he was caring for her. It seemed that he was a good deal smarter than she was in all things.

"Are you all right?" She nodded, then shook her head at Matt...Trevor. That was something else she was going to have to get used to. He was Trevor and not Matt, as they'd all thought. "I know just how you feel. It's like my life has been a lie and I just don't know where to start over or just let things go the way that they are now."

"I'm sorry about your parents, Trevor. They've been so close to you all this time, and you didn't know." He told her that he thought too that they'd been watching over him. "I don't doubt that at all. You're a good kid and smart too. They'd be so proud of you right now."

"You had a lot to do with my upbringing, Skye. I wouldn't have survived those first few years had you not taken me under your wing. You're the best mother figure a kid like me could have." She hugged him. Holding back tears as best she could, she held onto him until he pulled away. It occurred to her that she loved him like he really was her own son and wouldn't have had it any other way. "Don't get all emotional on me. You'll ruin my new shirt."

They both had a lot of new things. Not just clothing but a room for themselves. Food whenever they wanted it as well as someone to talk to in the way of the Savage family. All of them had been very good to them, and she couldn't have been happier to have them in their lives.

"Kaida saved my life, and I can't help but feel like I owe her everything. Did you hear that Tucker is looking into some contacts that he has to figure out what to do next? It's not like the Connors are going to be getting out of jail anytime soon. Nor will Jason." They had enough evidence on the Connors to keep them in jail as a flight risk. So far, they had demanded that the police allow them to take their son home and be done with everything. They weren't budging on allowing them to get out anytime soon.

Jason was going back to prison. This time, she hoped for good. The man had murdered more people than she would have imagined. And he'd been hired by the Connors to kill her and take the kid. How they figured out that she was with him, she might never know, but it was scary for her to think what he would have done to her had she not kept on the run from him.

"I think that we're safe for now, don't you?" She said that she'd never felt safer than she was right now. "Good. I was hoping you'd say that. Now, before you get upset with me, I'm going to go and see the Connors. They won't be in the same room as I will be, but far enough away from them that they can't touch me. Tucker said that he thinks I can get a confession from them where no one else will be able to."

"Please don't do this." He said that he needed some closure, too. "I would imagine that you do, but this isn't the way to go. They could hurt you. If not physically, then mentally, for sure."

"I started to tell you that I'd be fine, but I don't know that for sure. I do know that if I don't do this I'll wonder for the rest of my life as to why and how they did this to them and to me." He hugged her. "You can understand that, can't you? Why I'd need to know what made me so special at such a young age that they thought that they could get away with this. And they might well have if not for you coming along when you did."

They talked about other things in their life rather than the one that was going on now. She understood why he needed this and was happy that he could. However, she didn't have to like it any more than she was going to like confronting Jason someday in court. It was funny—not ha-ha funny but weird funny— how the two of them had found each other. If they hadn't, she was sure that at some point, she would have been murdered, and Trevor would be right back with the Connors being locked up in his room and only brought out when there was a way to show him off. Her heart hurt for the young boy.

When Tucker left with Trevor a few hours later, she went to the kitchen to find something to munch on until dinner. She didn't know what she was smelling, but she was looking forward to having whatever it was. This house always smelled like home-cooked meals and love. She envied the love that Kaida and Tucker had. It was like they were each in their own little world and only came out when it was impolite not to. She laughed every time she caught them kissing. It would embarrass them so much.

Getting to the police station an hour later, the time being set up by Jason's attorney, she sat outside his cell and watched him fumble around with his clothing. His attorney, someone she'd only just met, told her that she could ask him anything she wanted, but she wasn't to expect it to be used against him. Standing up, she was nearly to the door when she was called back.

"He told me that you'd be stubborn about this. Remember Ms. Houston, whether he agrees or not with that, everything is being recorded including there is a camera in every cell." He winked at her and she returned to the seat. "Now, she's only here because it was a request of yours to see her, Jason. What is it you wish to talk to her about?"

"Why couldn't you have just died?" Skye was startled by the questions. "It didn't matter what I did about you or to you, you just fucking wouldn't die. Christ, and I really tried, too. Everything that I did, you'd just get up and walk away."

"Maybe you just weren't as good as you thought you were." He said that he'd hired people to kill her, and they couldn't do it either. "I think a better question would be, why did you want me dead? I didn't know you at all. But you kept coming after me like you were stupid or something."

"I am not stupid, you fucking cunt. I've been killing women for decades, and you just wouldn't die." She asked him how many people he had killed. "Not people but lowlifes that owed someone something. I just wanted you dead, then one day, I saw you with that kid. I'd seen his picture someplace and went to the Connors about it. They didn't care what happened to you so long as they could get their boy back. Why did you kidnap their kid?"

"He wasn't their child. They killed his parents to get him." He snorted and told her that was why they were caught. Freelancing with murder is always going to get you caught. "Yet here you sit with bars around you caught too."

"You can't use this against me. I told you that." She shrugged and told him that she didn't care what he said. She'd use it if she was asked. "You fucking bitch. I swear to you, I hate people."

"I'm sure that not too many like you either. You're a murderer, liar, and a thief." She looked at the attorney, and he winked at her. "What did you want to talk to me about? I have a busy schedule and I need to keep on track of it."

"I hired someone to kill you soon. And when they do, I'm going to dance a little dance in happiness. You'll never be able to thrall him as you have me. He's a professional." She told him that he worked for the police. "No, I told you. I hired him right out of the jail cell before he got out."

"Right. He's working now, telling them everything you told them about me. In addition to things that you told him about me, you're also going to be tried for trying to kill off Trevor and the people who hired you to kill him. You tried to get them to pay up, and when they didn't, you —"

"No. He was in the jail cell right there. You don't know what you're talking about." She told him what he looked like. "No, you're wrong. Damn it. I know what I'm talking about." The door opened down the hall and she glanced in the direction of Brenin. He'd been in the jail cell next to Jason's and had recorded every word of what he wanted done to her. "That's him right there. See? I told…what is he

210 Kathi S. Barton

doing here?"

"He's my friend. And when they wanted you to confess to murder for hire, they asked him to come in and pretend to be a gun for hire. Didn't you think it was suspicious that he seemed more up on the laws than you did? Christ, you're an idiot of the first order, aren't you?"

Leaving this time, she let his shouts echo down the hallway where she was headed. Brenin asked her if she was all right and it was all she could do not to break down and fall on her face. As soon as she was outside, she sat on the steps and put her head between her knees.

"You told me what he said, but I didn't want to believe it. He was going to hire you to kill me." She looked up at him. "I know that you wouldn't have, but just the thought that he thought it was all right to hire someone to come along and kill me simply because he'd been asked to do it. I just don't understand where his mind was."

"He's probably been at killing for a good long time, and since he was never caught, he felt that he was doing something right. At least that's what I'm thinking." She asked him if he'd run into that sort of thing before. "I have. We all have. It's just the way that some people think about themselves. That they're something along the lines of the almighty and what they say and do is the way things should be done. I'm sorry that he hurt you, honey. Why don't you and I have some dinner and a nice cold beer and enjoy the rest of the day without thinking about Jason."

She took him up on his offer and wondered if Trevor was doing any better. She hoped so. The young man needed to have a good look on life before he got too much older and was jaded. Like her, he was all alone in the world, and she wanted nothing more than to keep him safe and happy for the rest of their lives.

AWARD WINNING, BESTSELLING AUTHOR

Kathi Barton, a winner of the Pinnacle Book Achievement Award and a best-selling author on Amazon and All Romance books, lives in Nashport, Ohio, with her husband, Paul. When not creating new worlds and romance, Kathi and her husband enjoy camping and going to auctions. She can also be seen at county fairs with her husband, an artist and potter.

Her muse, a cross between Jimmy Stewart and Hugh Jackman, brings her stories to life for her readers in a way that has them coming back time and again for more. Her favorite genre is paranormal romance, with a great deal of spice. You can visit Kathi online and drop her an email if you'd like. She loves hearing from her fans. aaronskiss@gmail.com.

Follow Kathi on her blog: http://kathisbartonauthor.blogspot.com/

www.ingramcontent.com/pod-product-compliance
Lightning Source LLC
Chambersburg PA
CBHW031955170626
46807CB00006B/2498